FOX & RABBIT

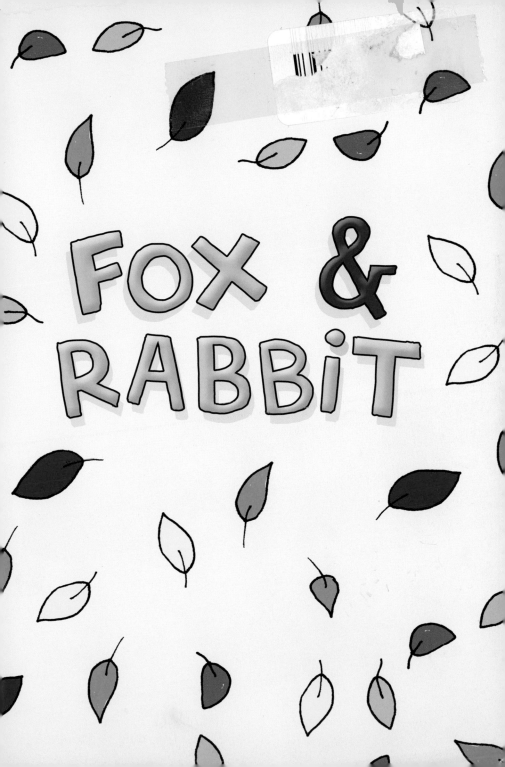

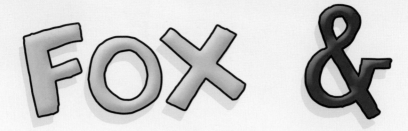

FOX &

MAKE BELIEVE

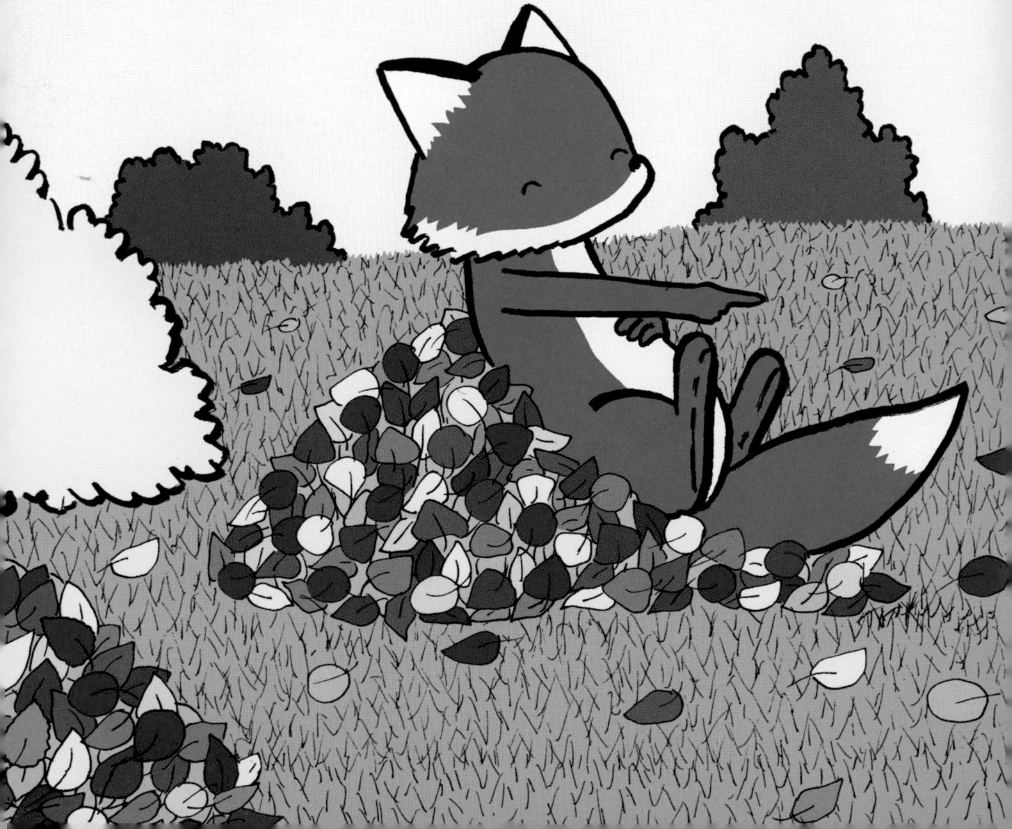

RABBiT

by Beth Ferry

illustrated by Gergely Dudás

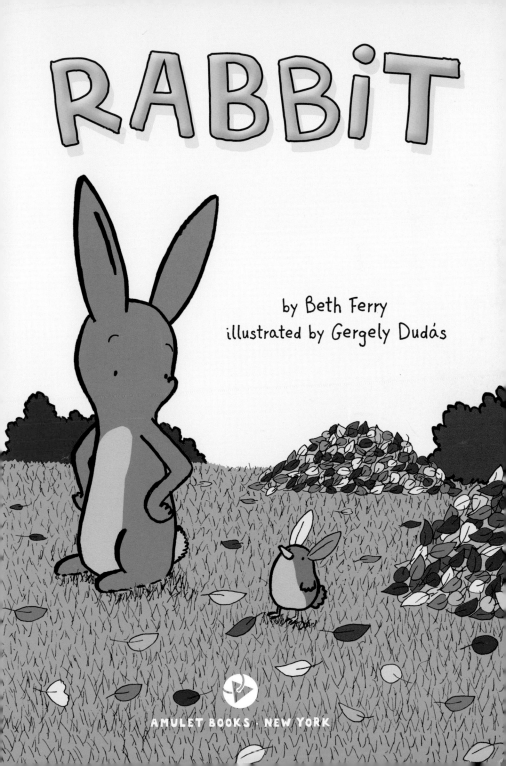

AMULET BOOKS · NEW YORK

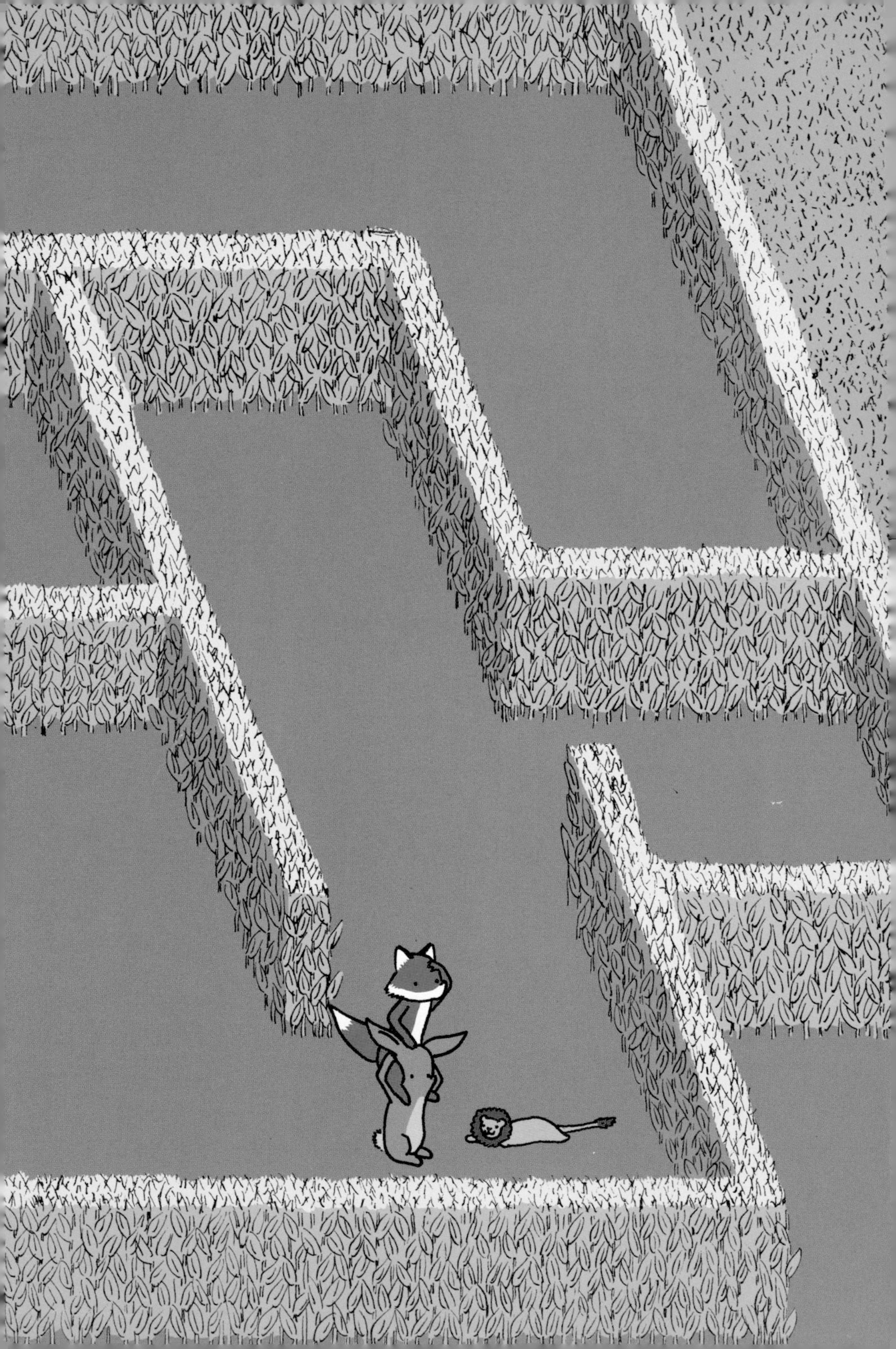

CONTENTS

MONEY, MARSHMALLOWS & MMMMMM

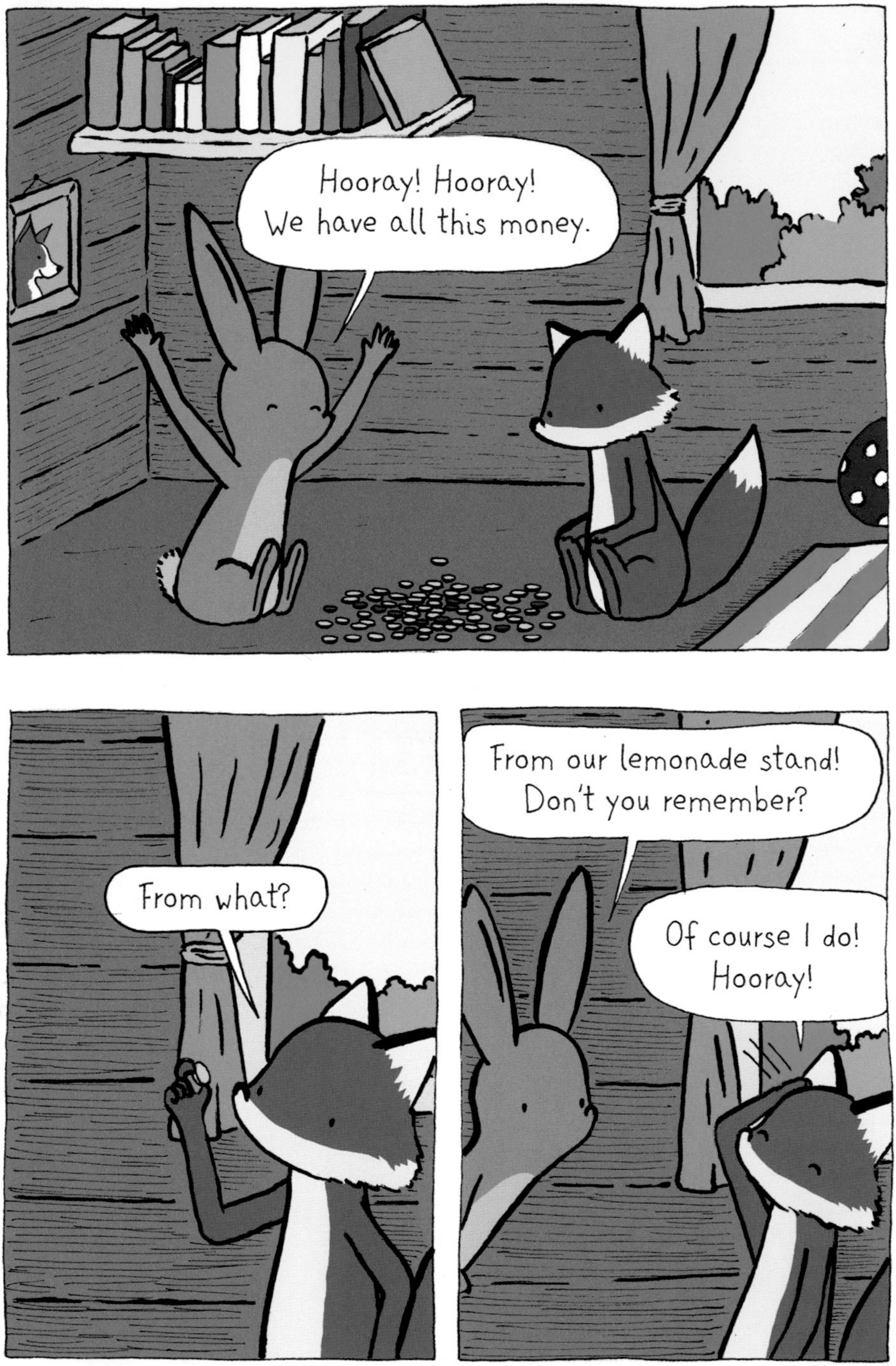
Hooray! Hooray!
We have all this money.
From what?
From our lemonade stand!
Don't you remember?
Of course I do!
Hooray!

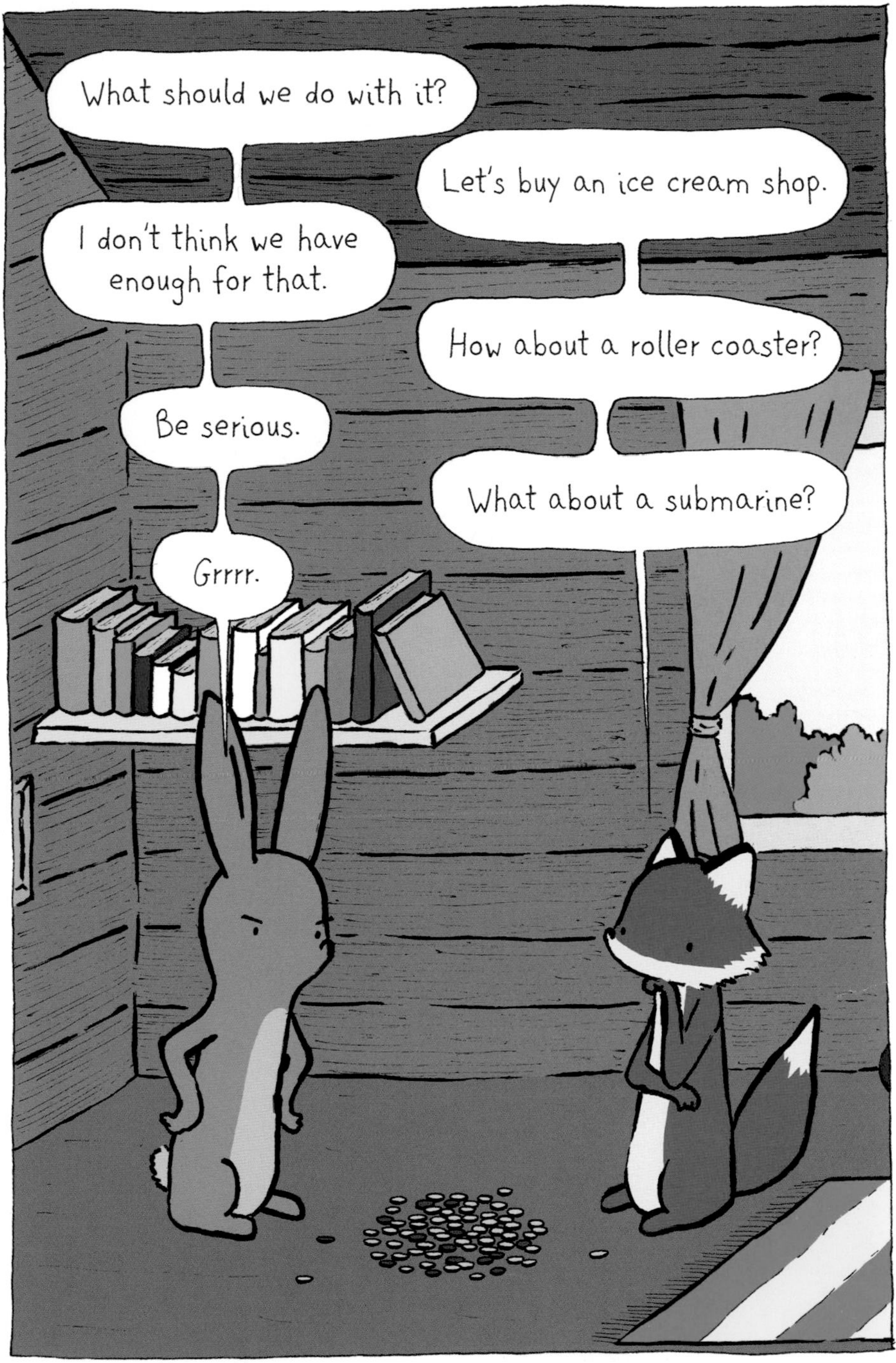
What should we do with it?
Let's buy an ice cream shop.
I don't think we have enough for that.
How about a roller coaster?
Be serious.
What about a submarine?
Grrrr.

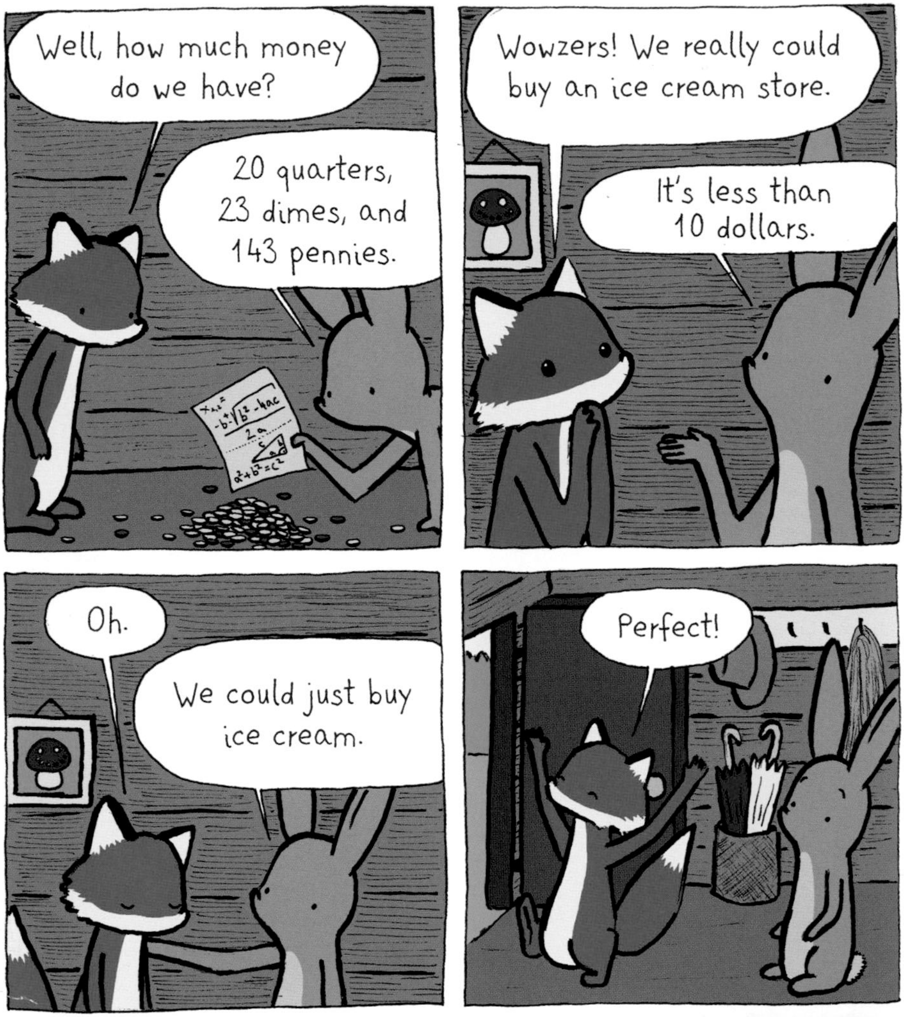
Well, how much money do we have?
20 quarters, 23 dimes, and 143 pennies.
Wowzers! We really could buy an ice cream store.
It's less than 10 dollars.
Oh.
We could just buy ice cream.
Perfect!

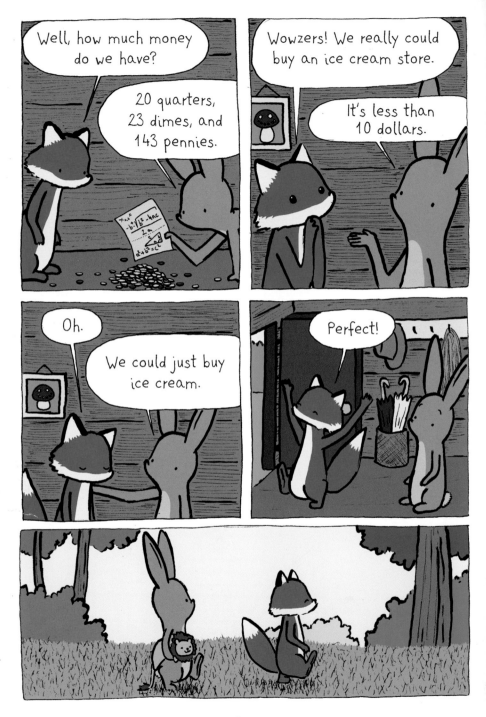

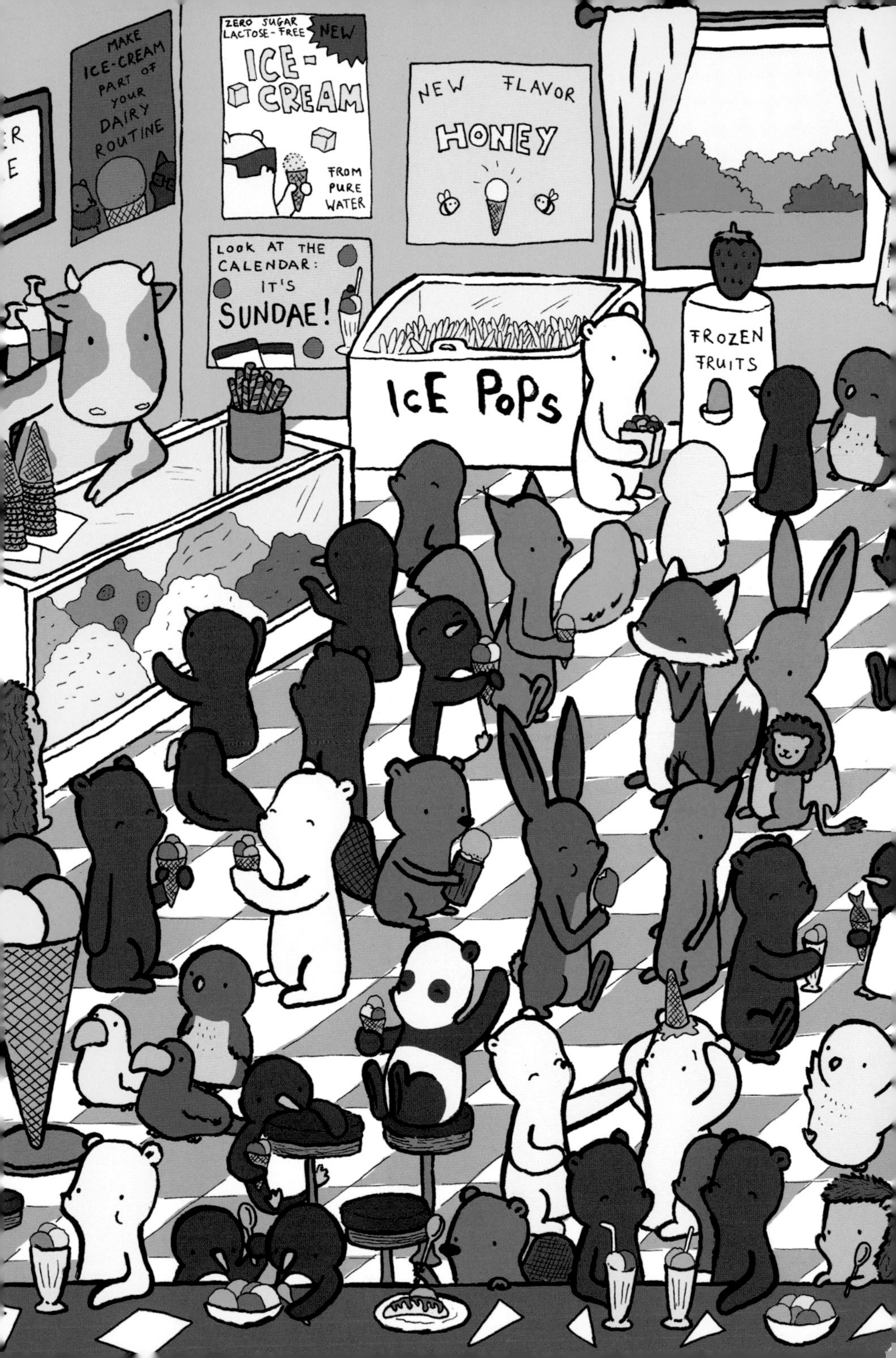
MAKE ICE-CREAM PART OF YOUR DAIRY ROUTINE
ZERO SUGAR LACTOSE-FREE
NEW
ICE-CREAM
FROM PURE WATER
NEW FLAVOR
HONEY
LOOK AT THE CALENDAR: IT'S SUNDAE!
IcE PoPs
FROZEN FRUITS

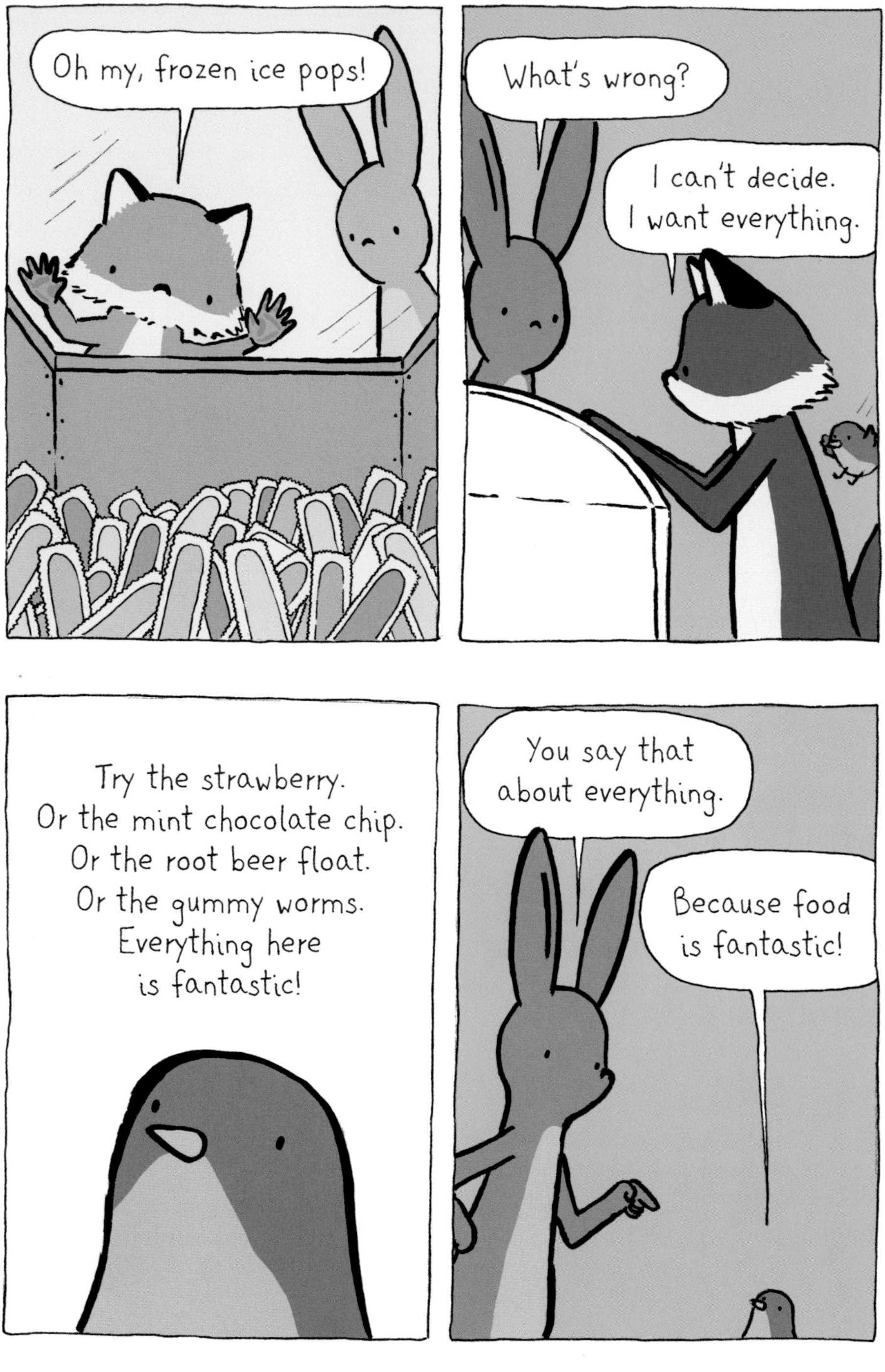
Oh my, frozen ice pops!
What's wrong?
I can't decide. I want everything.
Try the strawberry. Or the mint chocolate chip. Or the root beer float. Or the gummy worms. Everything here is fantastic!
You say that about everything.
Because food is fantastic!

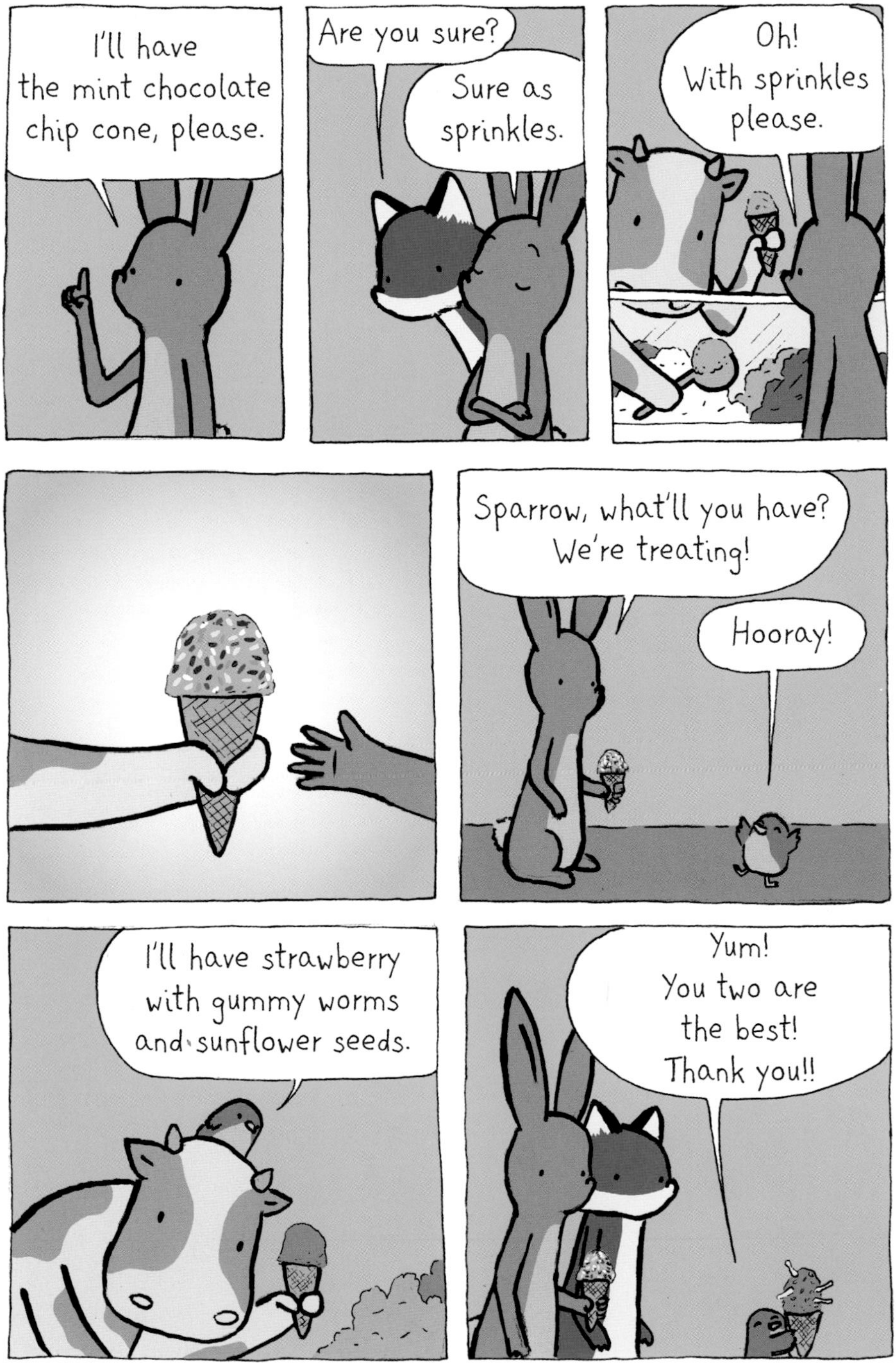
I'll have
the mint chocolate
chip cone, please.
Are you sure?
Sure as
sprinkles.
Oh!
With sprinkles
please.
Sparrow, what'll you have?
We're treating!
Hooray!
I'll have strawberry
with gummy worms
and sunflower seeds.
Yum!
You two are
the best!
Thank you!!

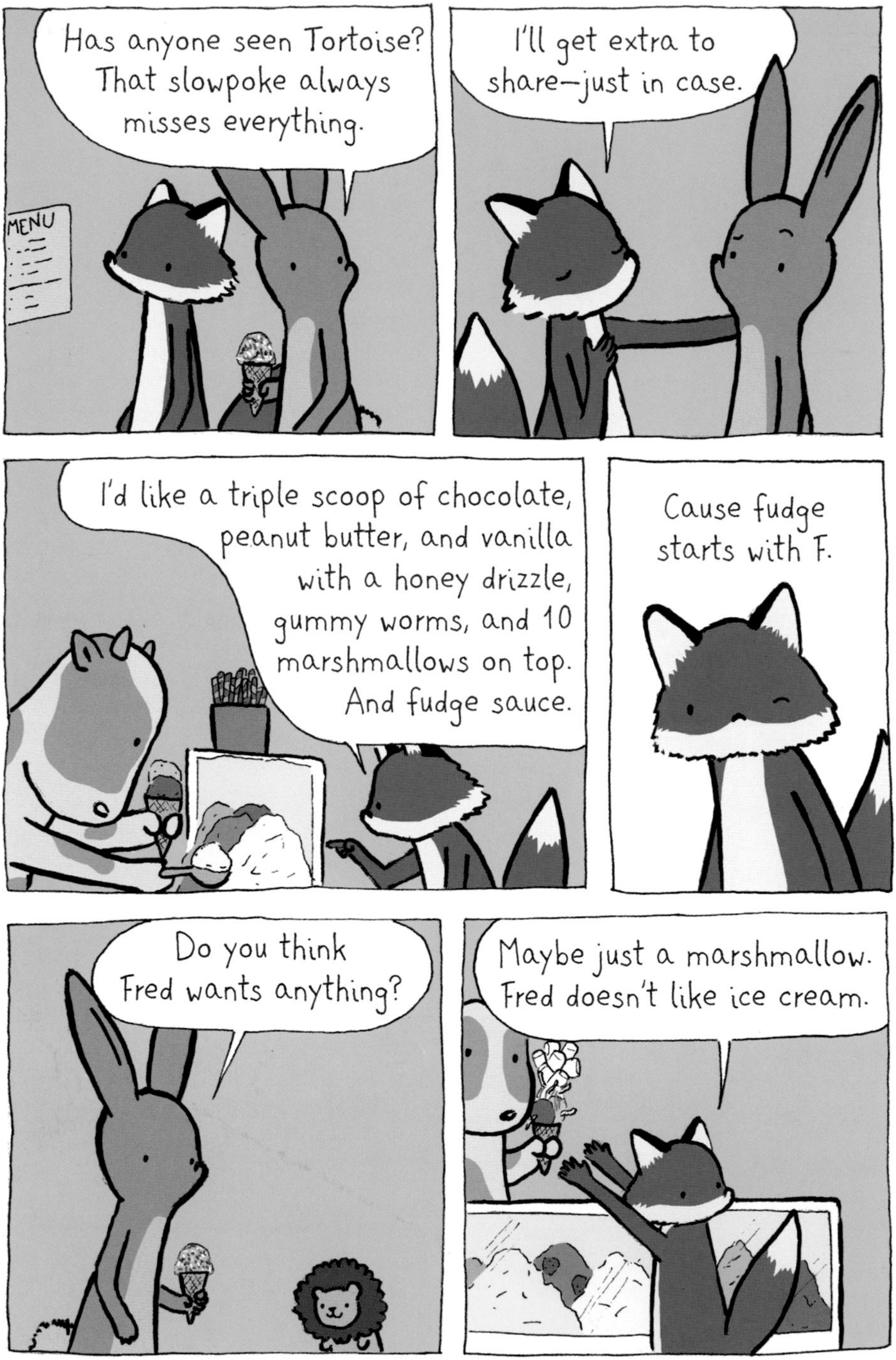
Has anyone seen Tortoise? That slowpoke always misses everything.
MENU
I'll get extra to share—just in case.
I'd like a triple scoop of chocolate, peanut butter, and vanilla with a honey drizzle, gummy worms, and 10 marshmallows on top. And fudge sauce.
Cause fudge starts with F.
Do you think Fred wants anything?
Maybe just a marshmallow. Fred doesn't like ice cream.

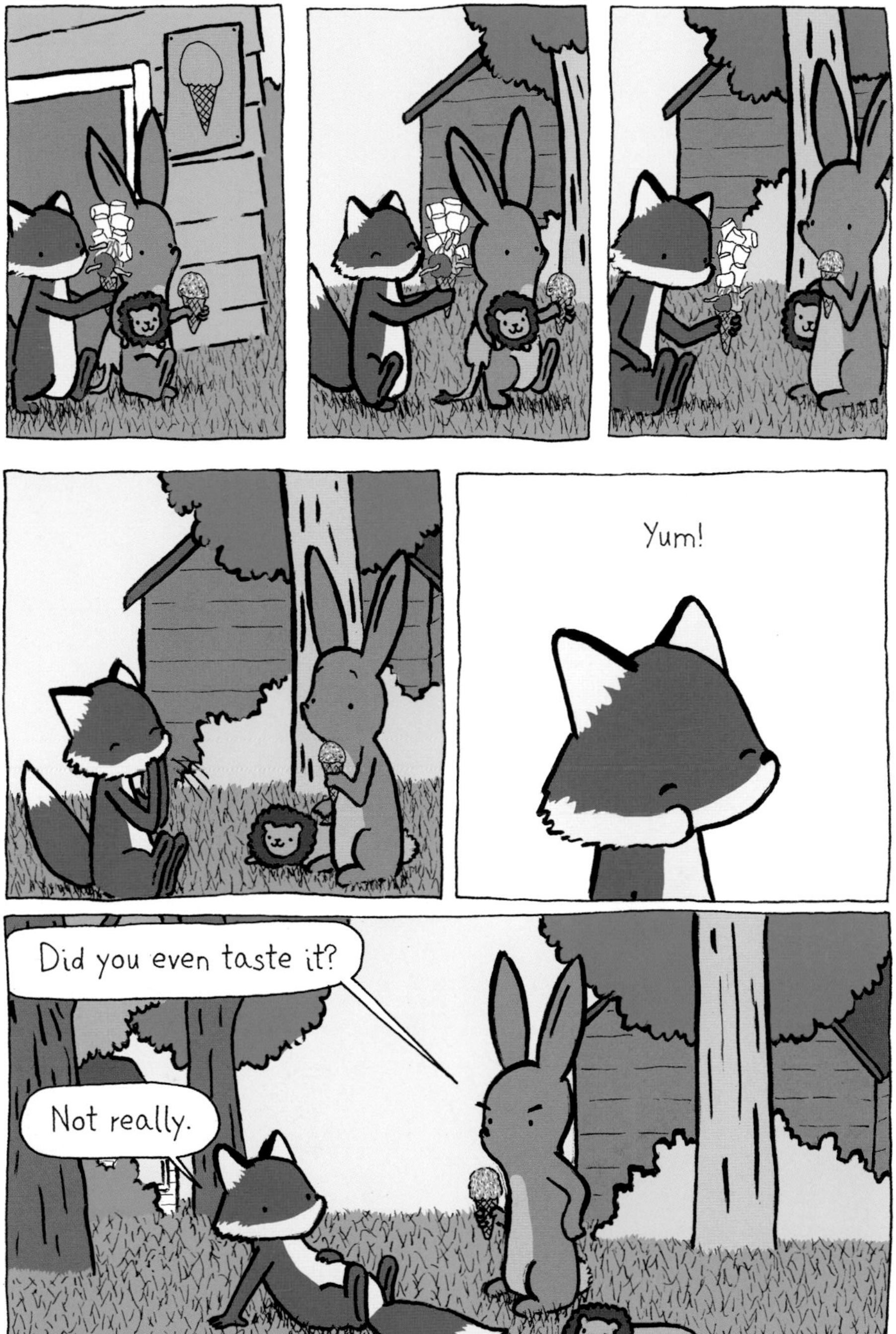
Yum!
Did you even taste it?
Not really.

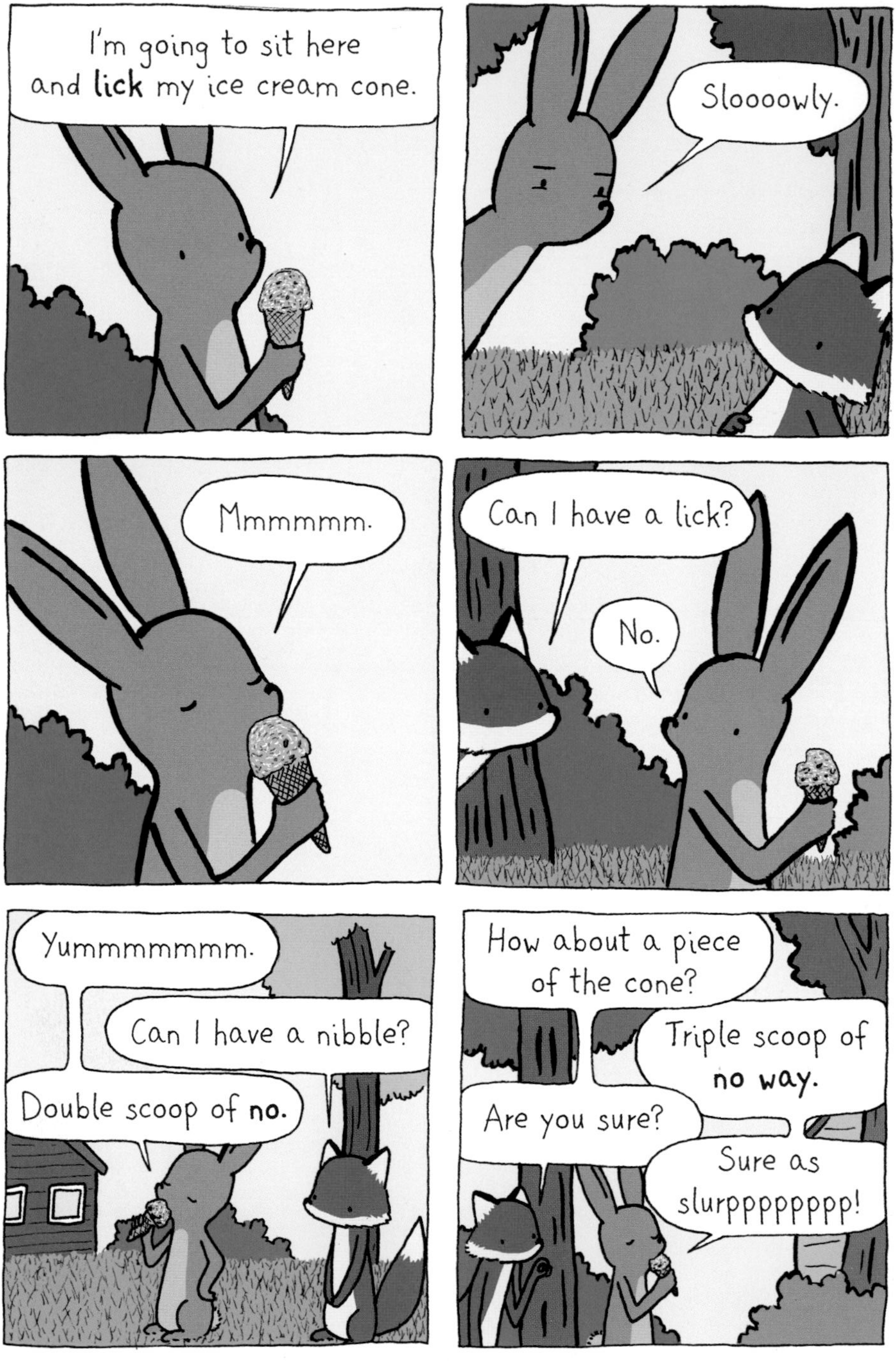
I'm going to sit here
and **lick** my ice cream cone.
Sloooowly.
Mmmmmm.
Can I have a lick?
No.
Yummmmmmm.
Can I have a nibble?
Double scoop of **no.**
How about a piece
of the cone?
Triple scoop of
no way.
Are you sure?
Sure as
slurppppppp!

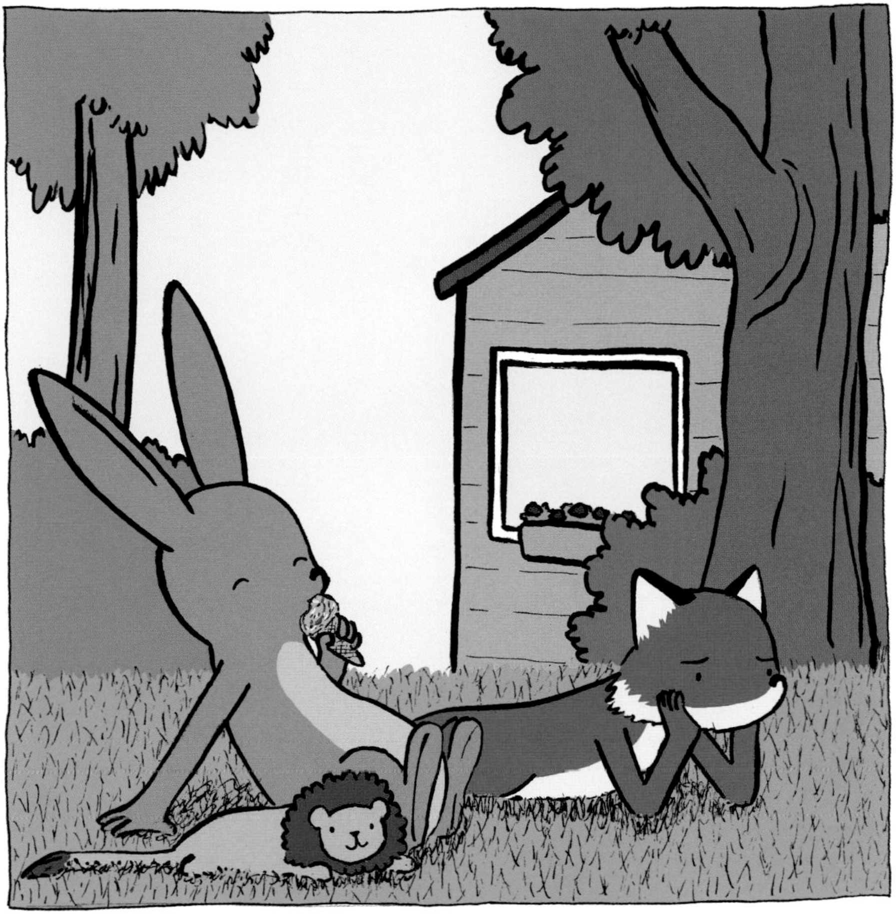

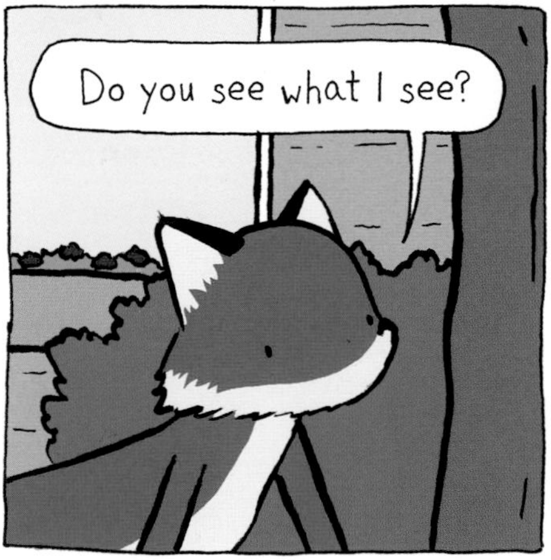
Do you see what I see?

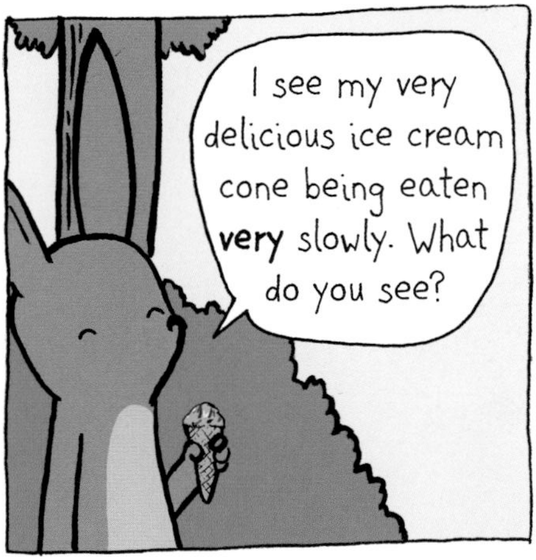
I see my very delicious ice cream cone being eaten **very** slowly. What do you see?

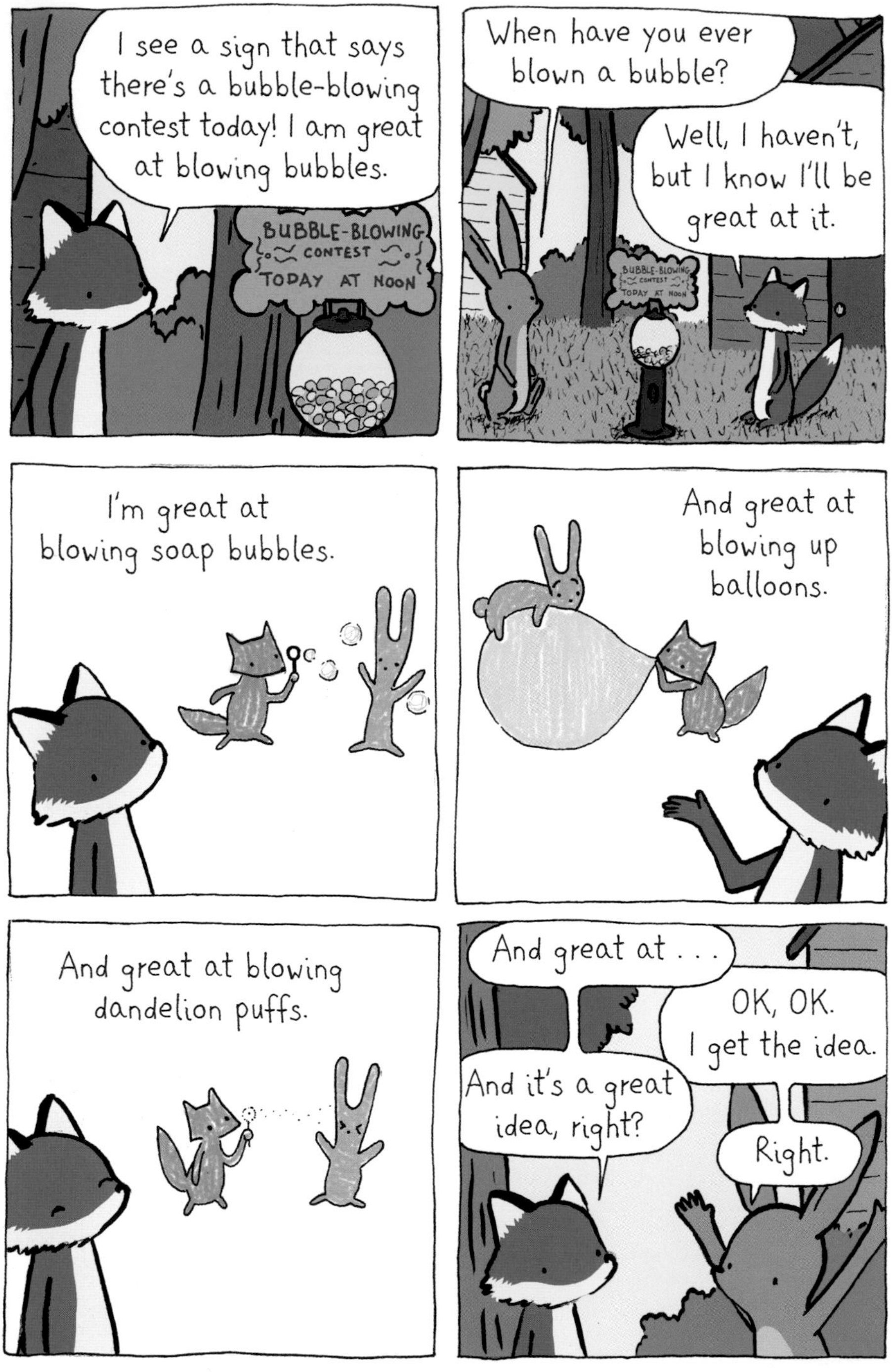
I see a sign that says there's a bubble-blowing contest today! I am great at blowing bubbles.
BUBBLE-BLOWING CONTEST TODAY AT NOON
When have you ever blown a bubble?
Well, I haven't, but I know I'll be great at it.
BUBBLE-BLOWING CONTEST TODAY AT NOON
I'm great at blowing soap bubbles.
And great at blowing up balloons.
And great at blowing dandelion puffs.
And great at . . .
OK, OK. I get the idea.
And it's a great idea, right?
Right.

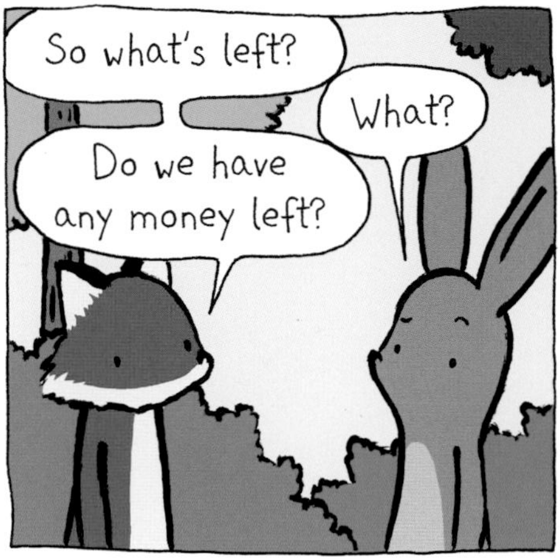
So what's left?
Do we have any money left?
What?

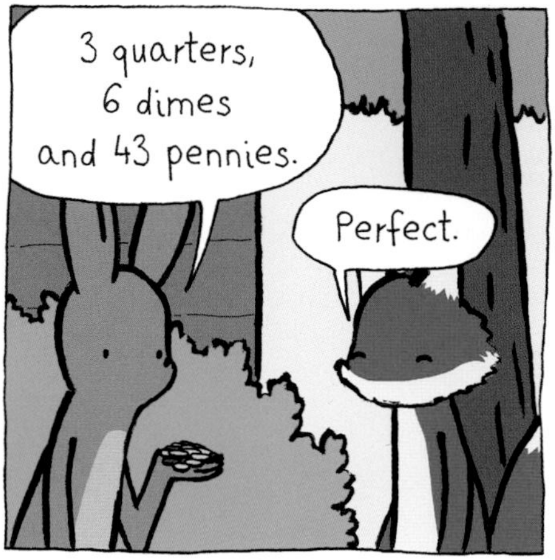
3 quarters, 6 dimes and 43 pennies.
Perfect.

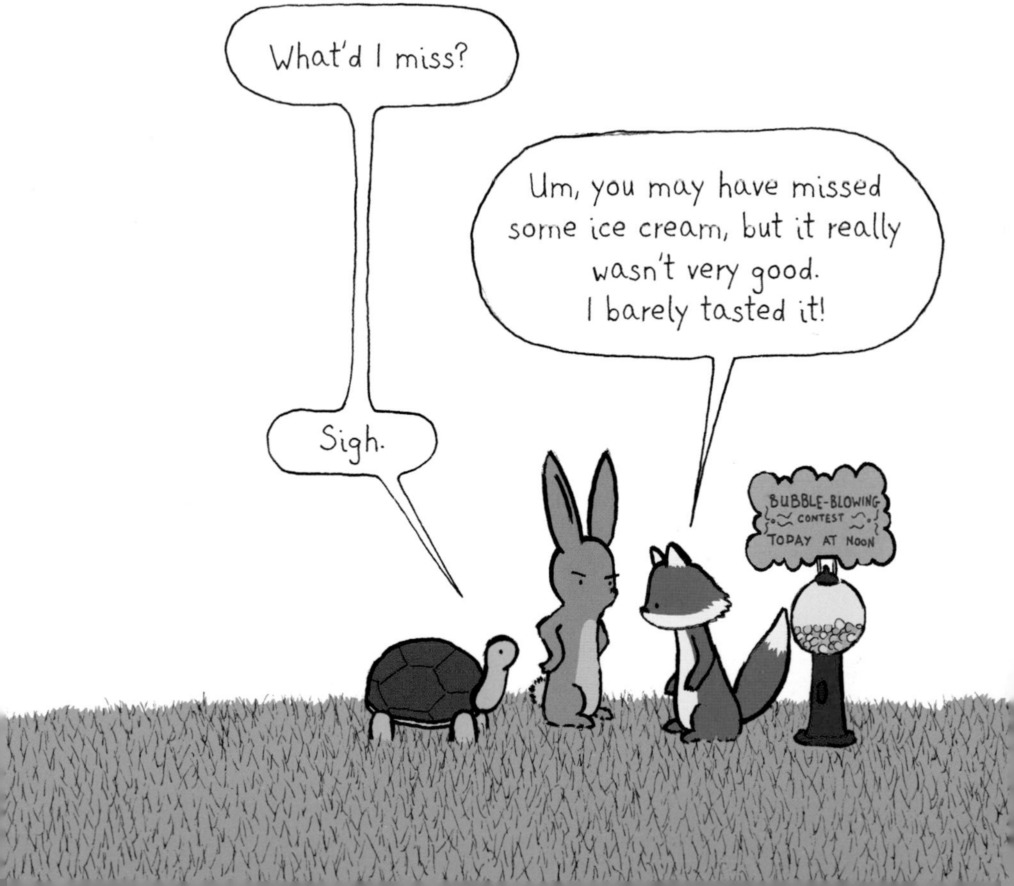
What'd I miss?
Sigh.
Um, you may have missed some ice cream, but it really wasn't very good. I barely tasted it!
BUBBLE-BLOWING CONTEST TODAY AT NOON

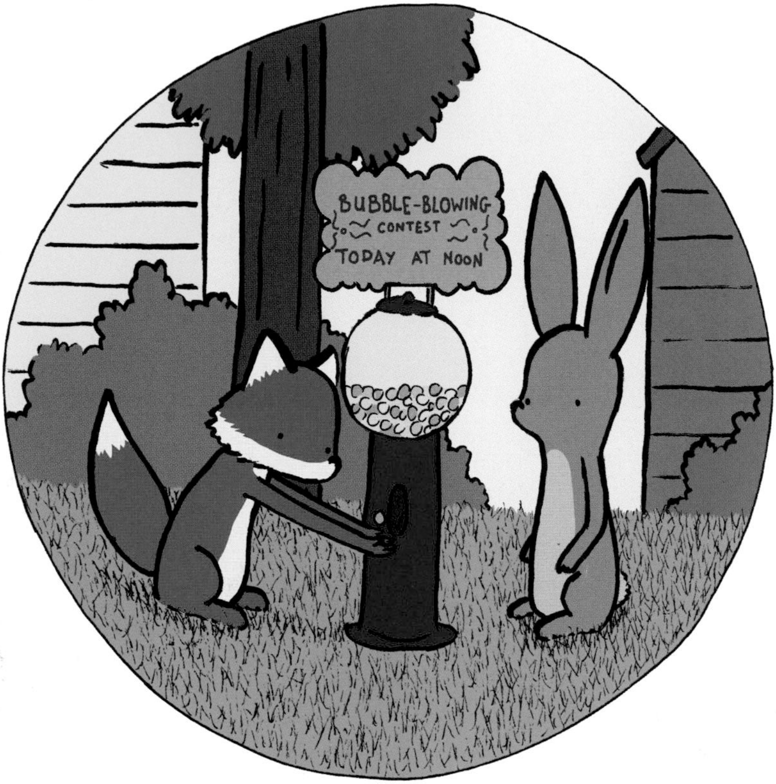
BUBBLE-BLOWING
CONTEST
TODAY AT NOON

STORY TWO

GUM, YUM & CHUM

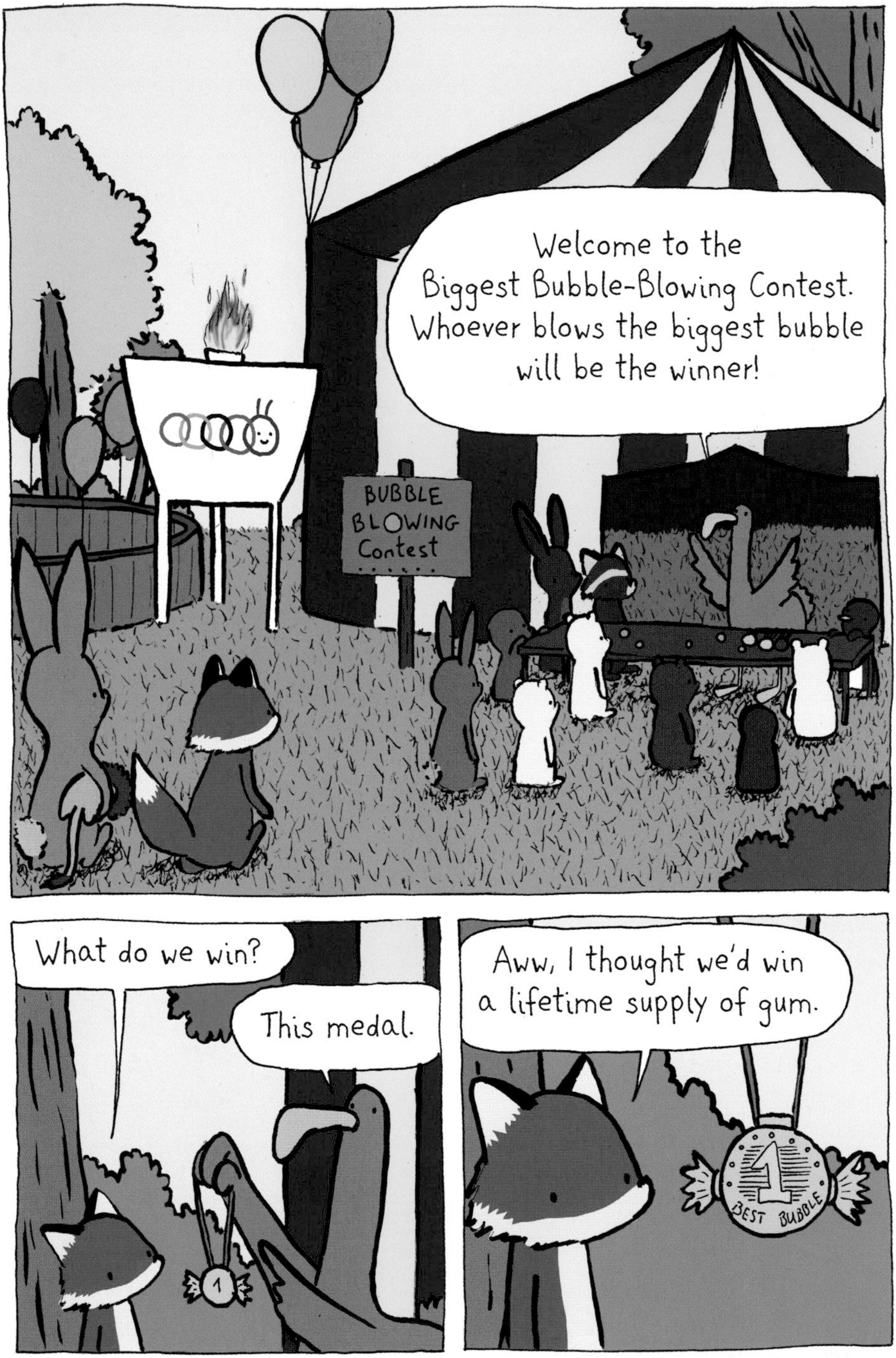
Welcome to the Biggest Bubble-Blowing Contest. Whoever blows the biggest bubble will be the winner!
BUBBLE BLOWING Contest
What do we win?
This medal.
Aww, I thought we'd win a lifetime supply of gum.
1
BEST BUBBLE

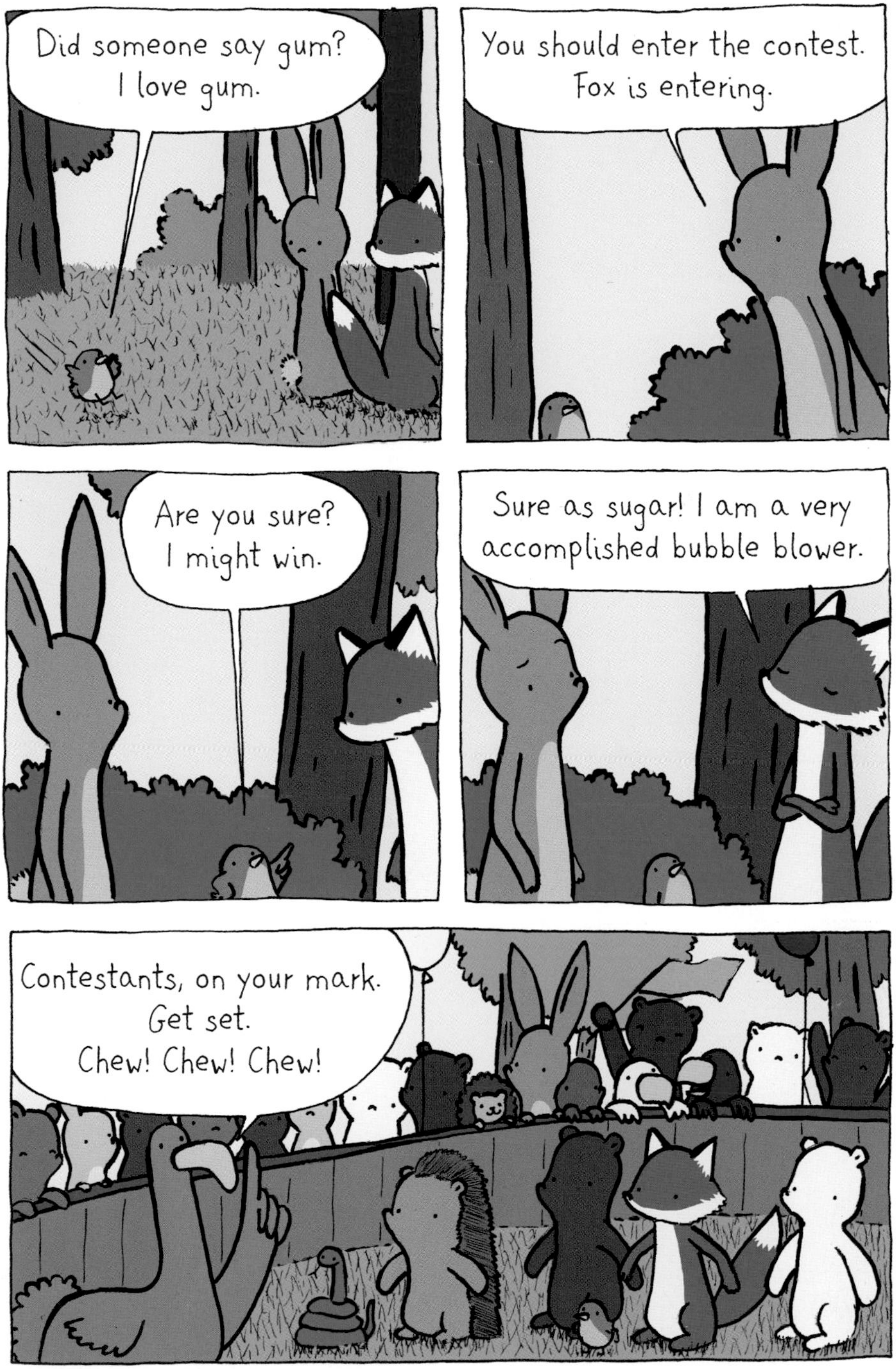
Did someone say gum?
I love gum.
You should enter the contest.
Fox is entering.
Are you sure?
I might win.
Sure as sugar! I am a very
accomplished bubble blower.
Contestants, on your mark.
Get set.
Chew! Chew! Chew!

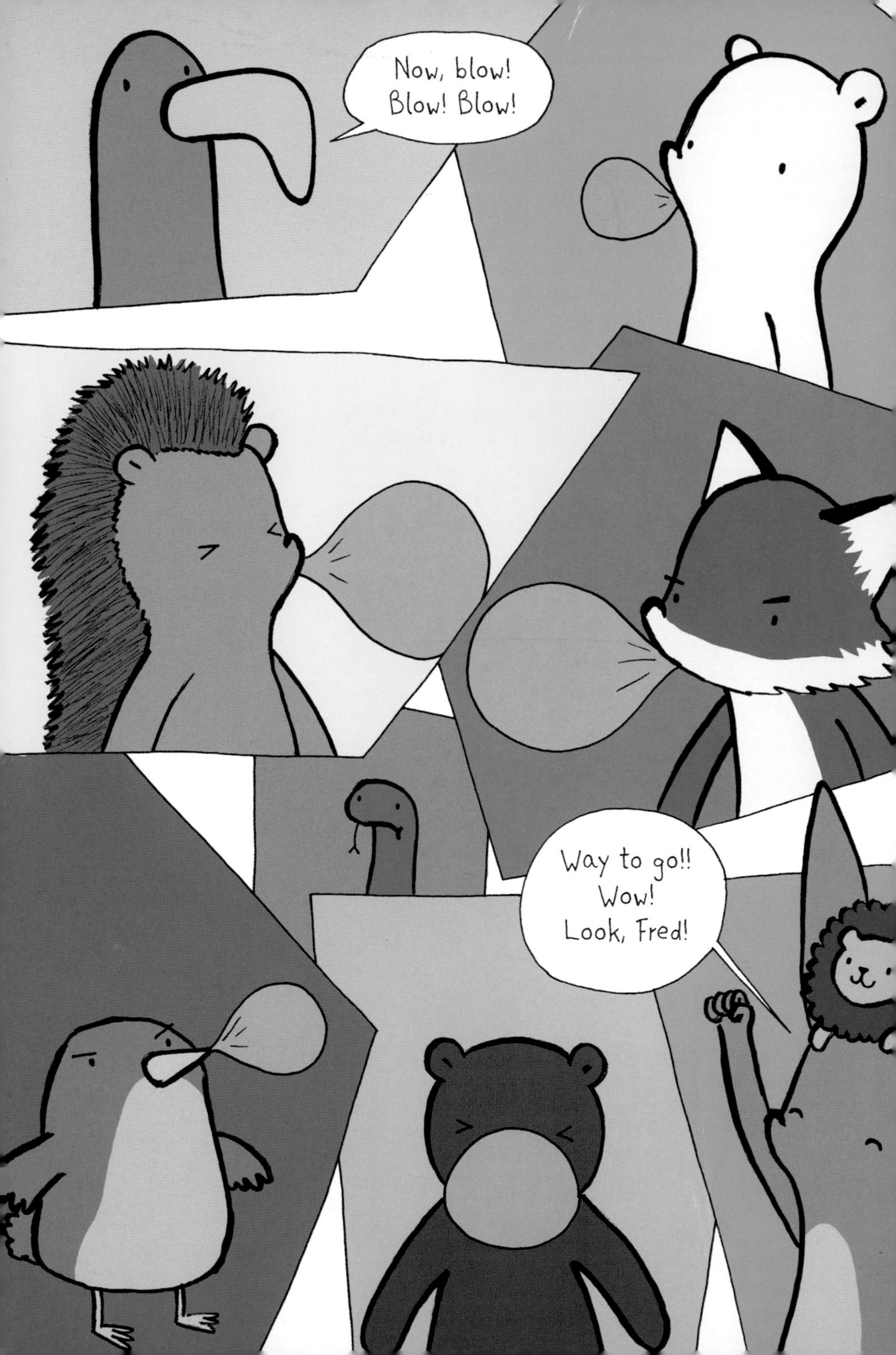
Now, blow!
Blow! Blow!
Way to go!!
Wow!
Look, Fred!

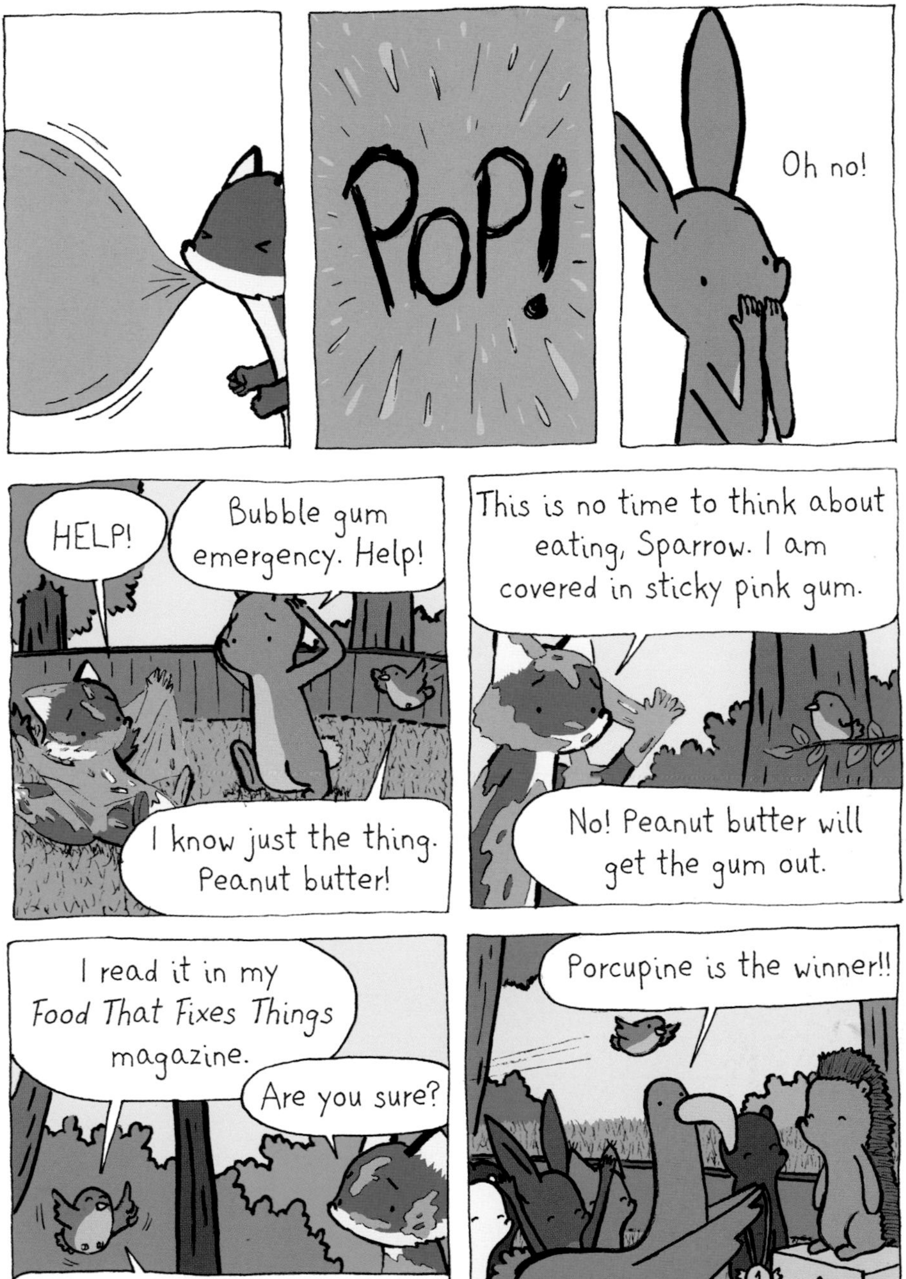
POP!
Oh no!
HELP!
Bubble gum emergency. Help!
I know just the thing. Peanut butter!
This is no time to think about eating, Sparrow. I am covered in sticky pink gum.
No! Peanut butter will get the gum out.
I read it in my *Food That Fixes Things* magazine.
Are you sure?
Sure as super creamy peanut butter! I'll be back in a jiff!
Porcupine is the winner!!
1
2
1

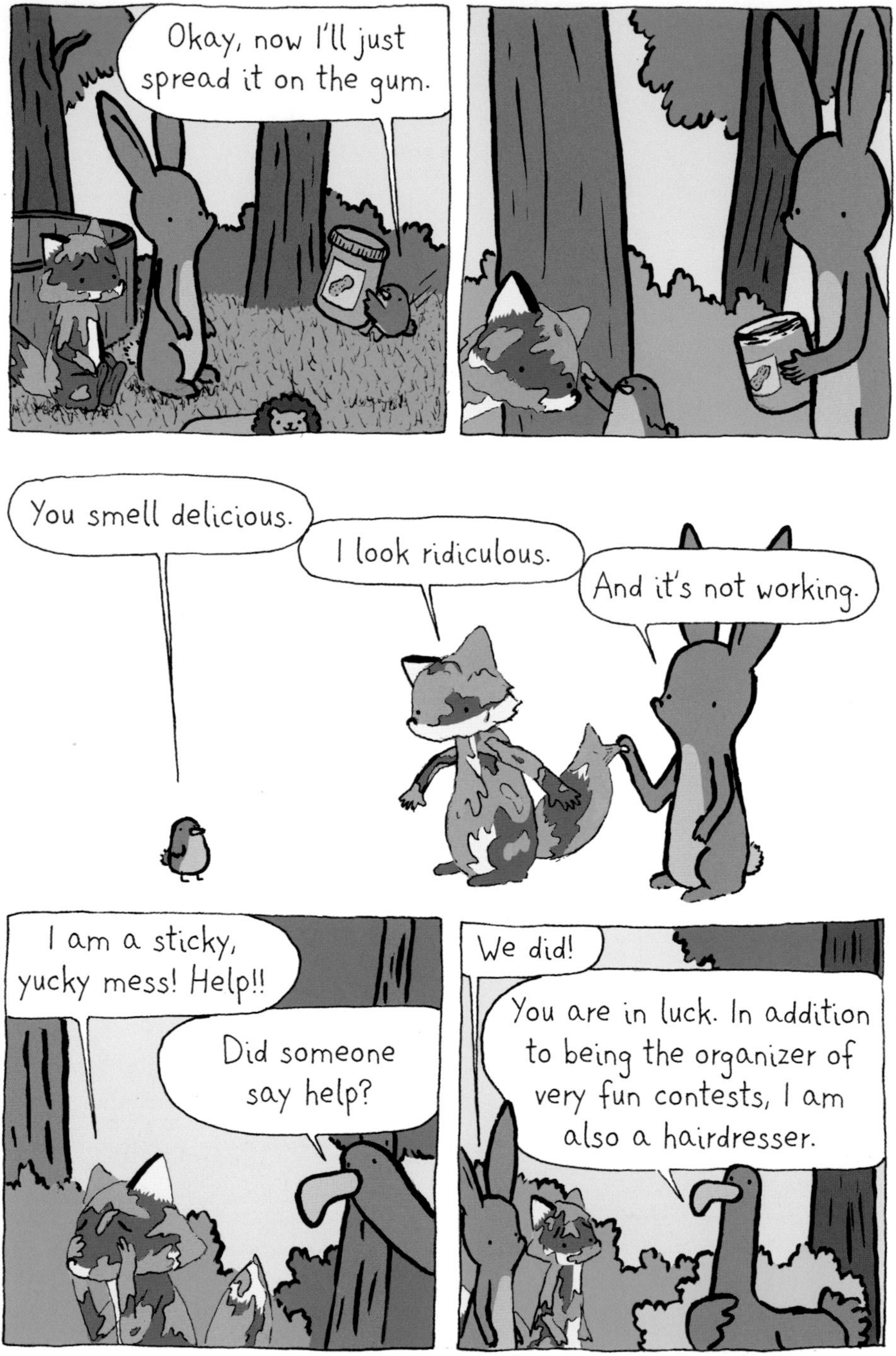

Okay, now I'll just spread it on the gum.
You smell delicious.
I look ridiculous.
And it's not working.
I am a sticky, yucky mess! Help!!
Did someone say help?
We did!
You are in luck. In addition to being the organizer of very fun contests, I am also a hairdresser.

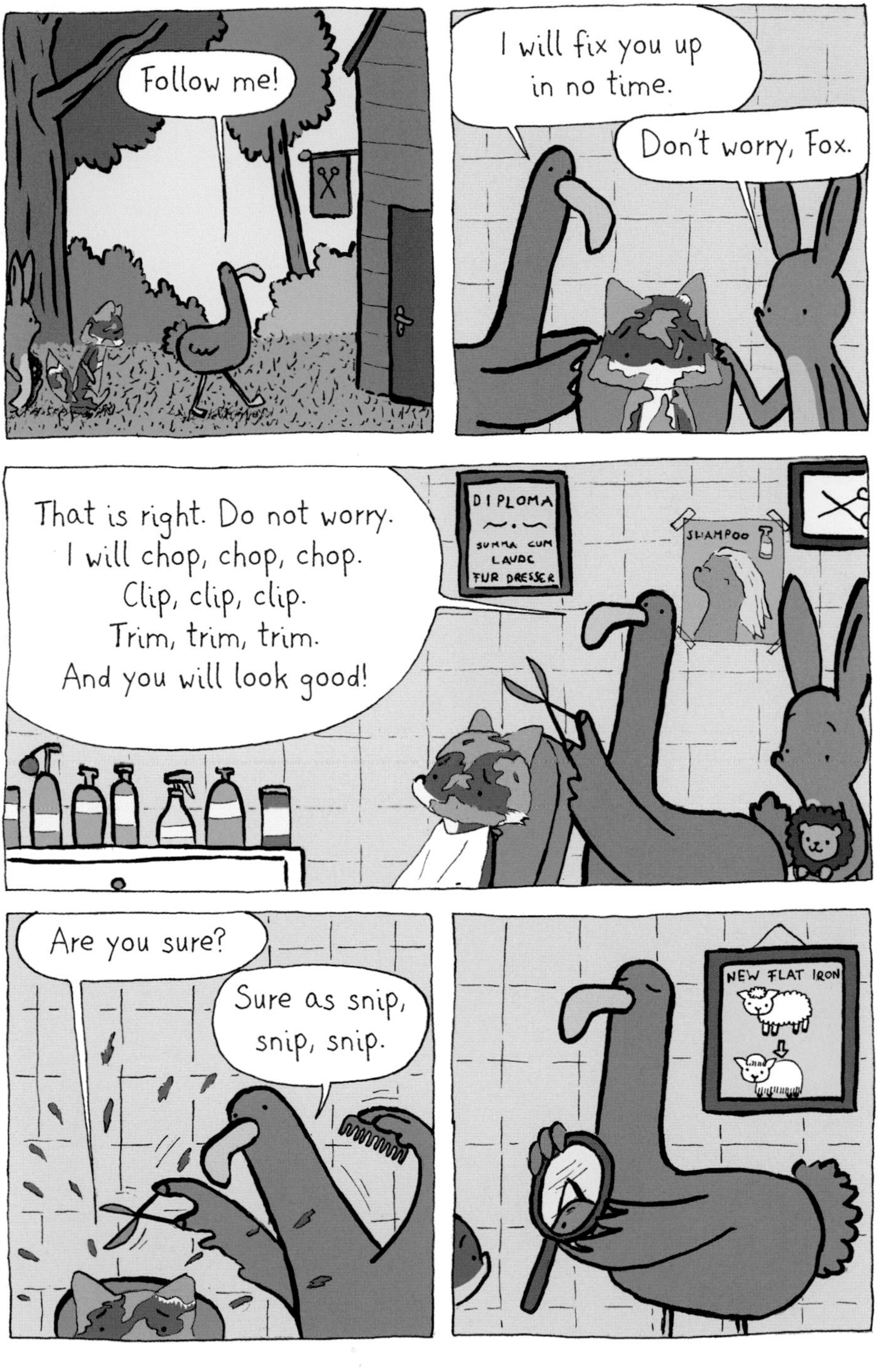
Follow me!
I will fix you up in no time.
Don't worry, Fox.
That is right. Do not worry. I will chop, chop, chop. Clip, clip, clip. Trim, trim, trim. And you will look good!
DIPLOMA
SUMMA CUM LAUDE FUR DRESSER
SHAMPOO
Are you sure?
Sure as snip, snip, snip.
NEW FLAT IRON

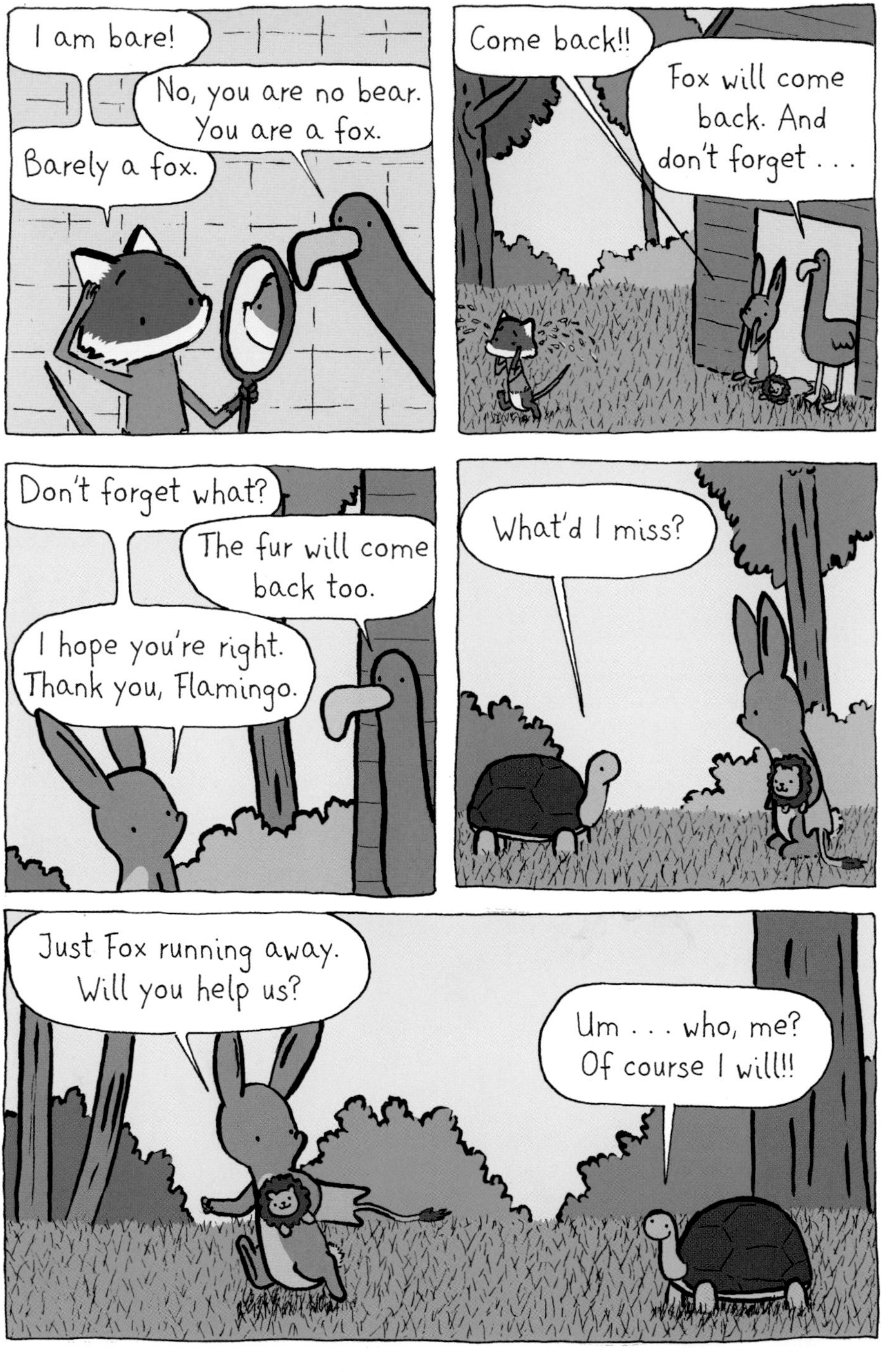
I am bare!
No, you are no bear. You are a fox.
Barely a fox.
Come back!!
Fox will come back. And don't forget . . .
Don't forget what?
The fur will come back too.
I hope you're right. Thank you, Flamingo.
What'd I miss?
Just Fox running away. Will you help us?
Um . . . who, me? Of course I will!!

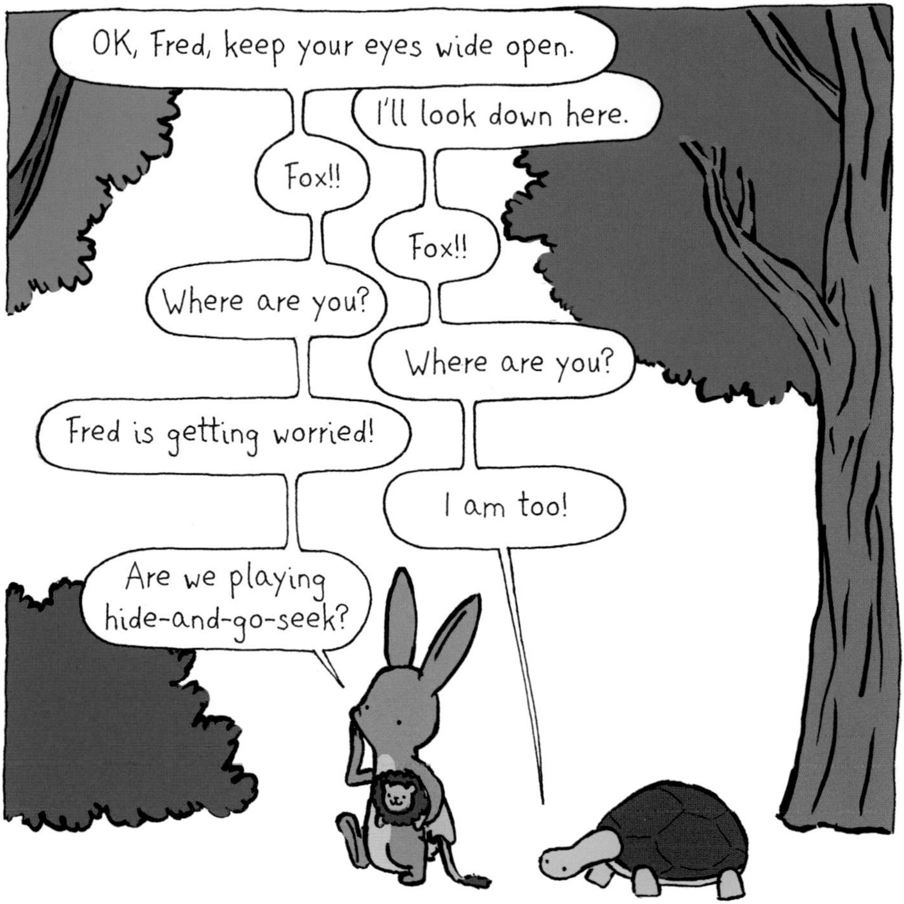
OK, Fred, keep your eyes wide open.
I'll look down here.
Fox!!
Fox!!
Where are you?
Where are you?
Fred is getting worried!
I am too!
Are we playing hide-and-go-seek?

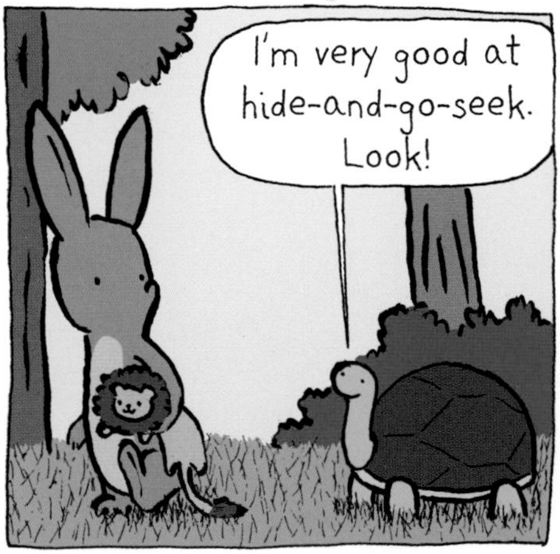
I'm very good at hide-and-go-seek. Look!

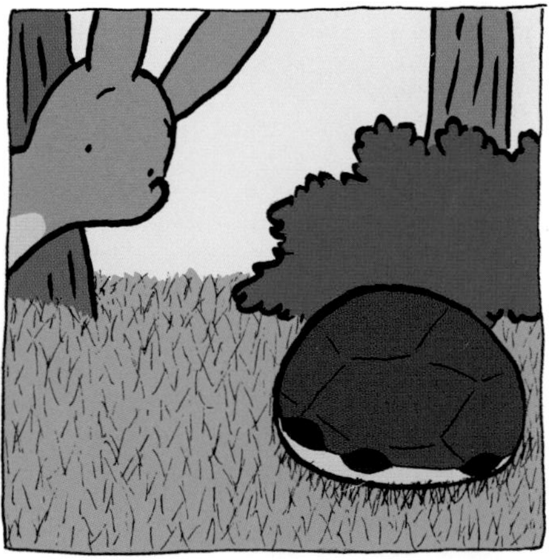

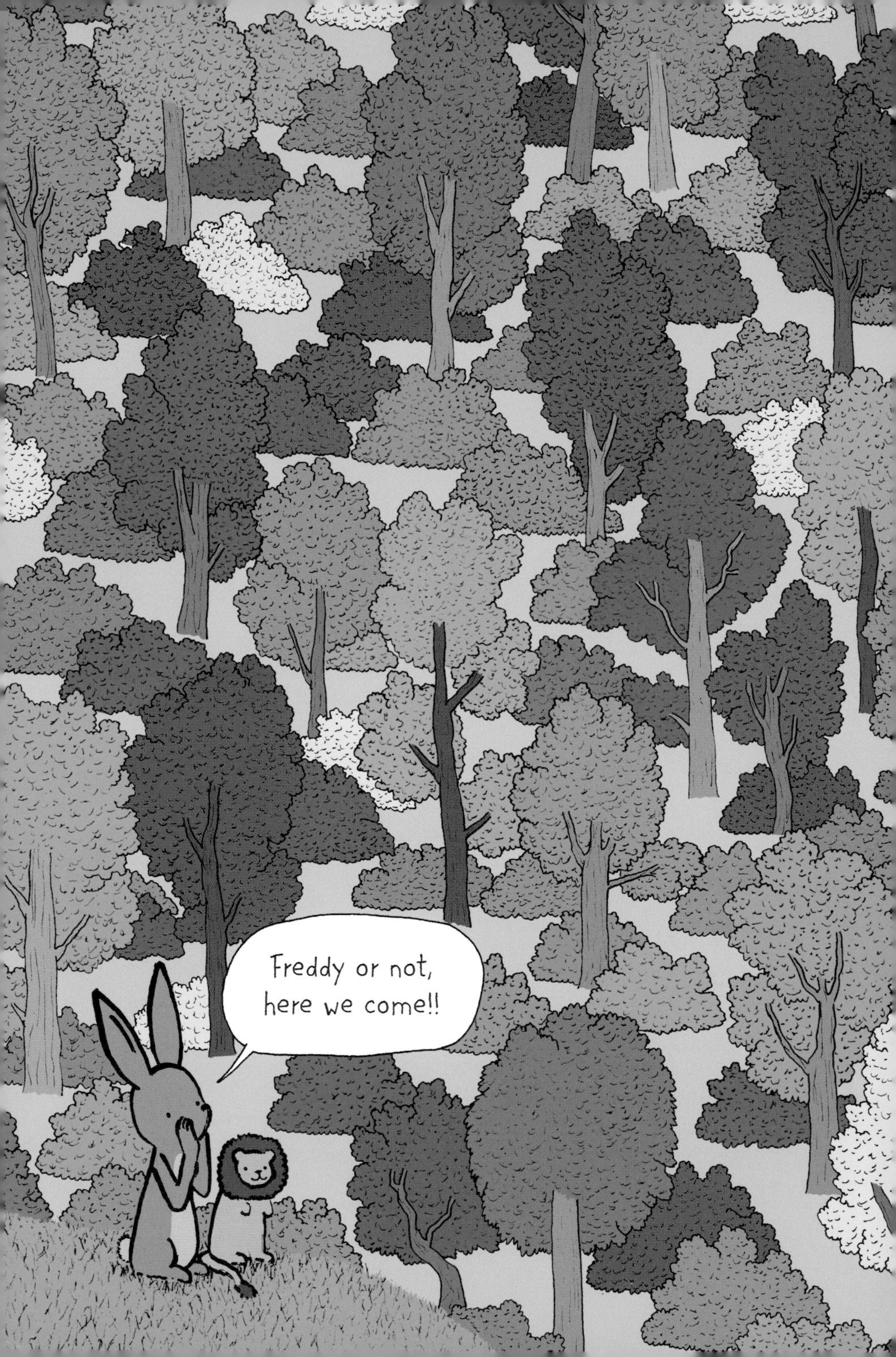
Freddy or not, here we come!!

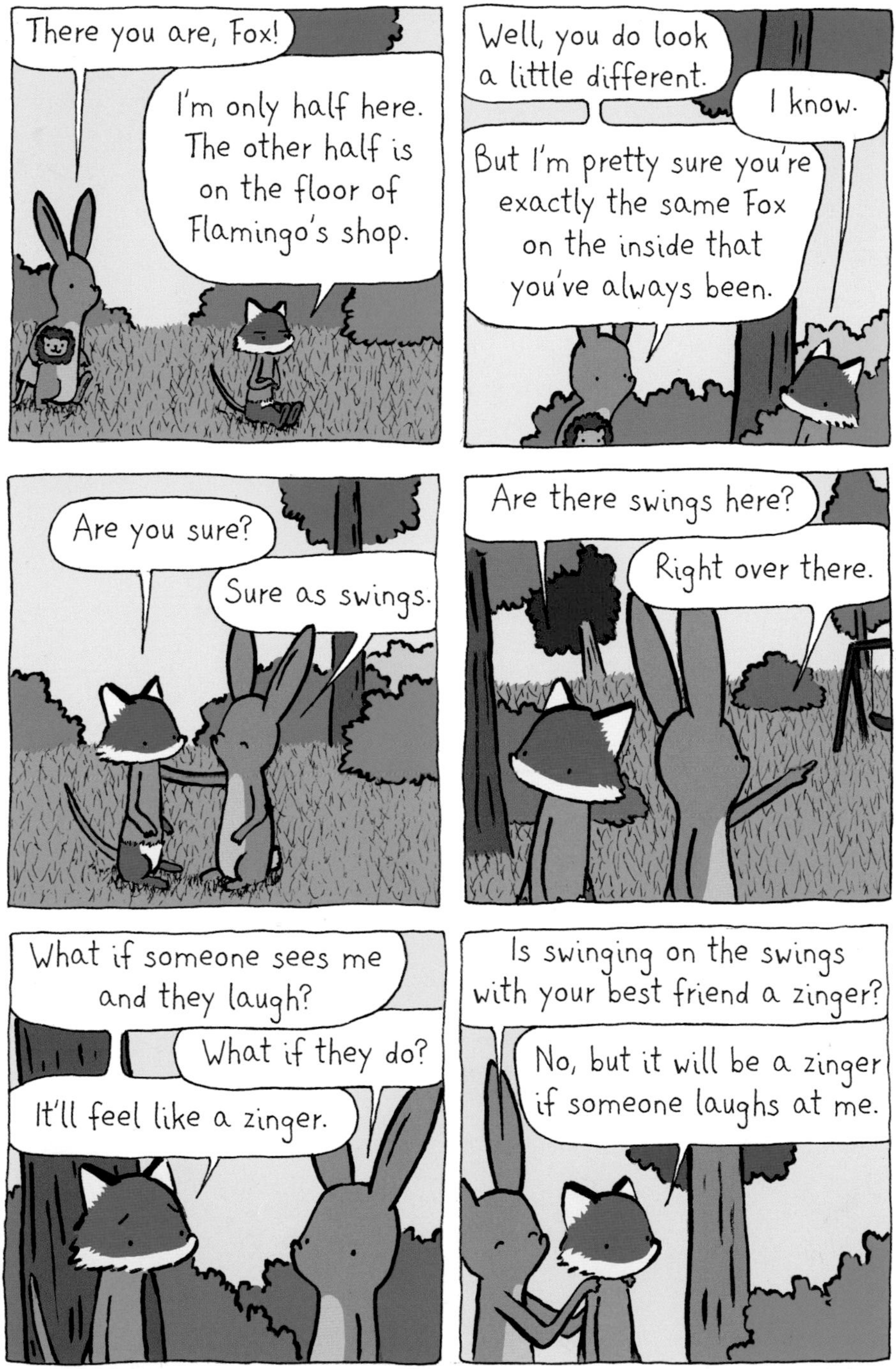
There you are, Fox!
I'm only half here. The other half is on the floor of Flamingo's shop.
Well, you do look a little different.
But I'm pretty sure you're exactly the same Fox on the inside that you've always been.
I know.
Are you sure?
Sure as swings.
Are there swings here?
Right over there.
What if someone sees me and they laugh?
What if they do?
It'll feel like a zinger.
Is swinging on the swings with your best friend a zinger?
No, but it will be a zinger if someone laughs at me.

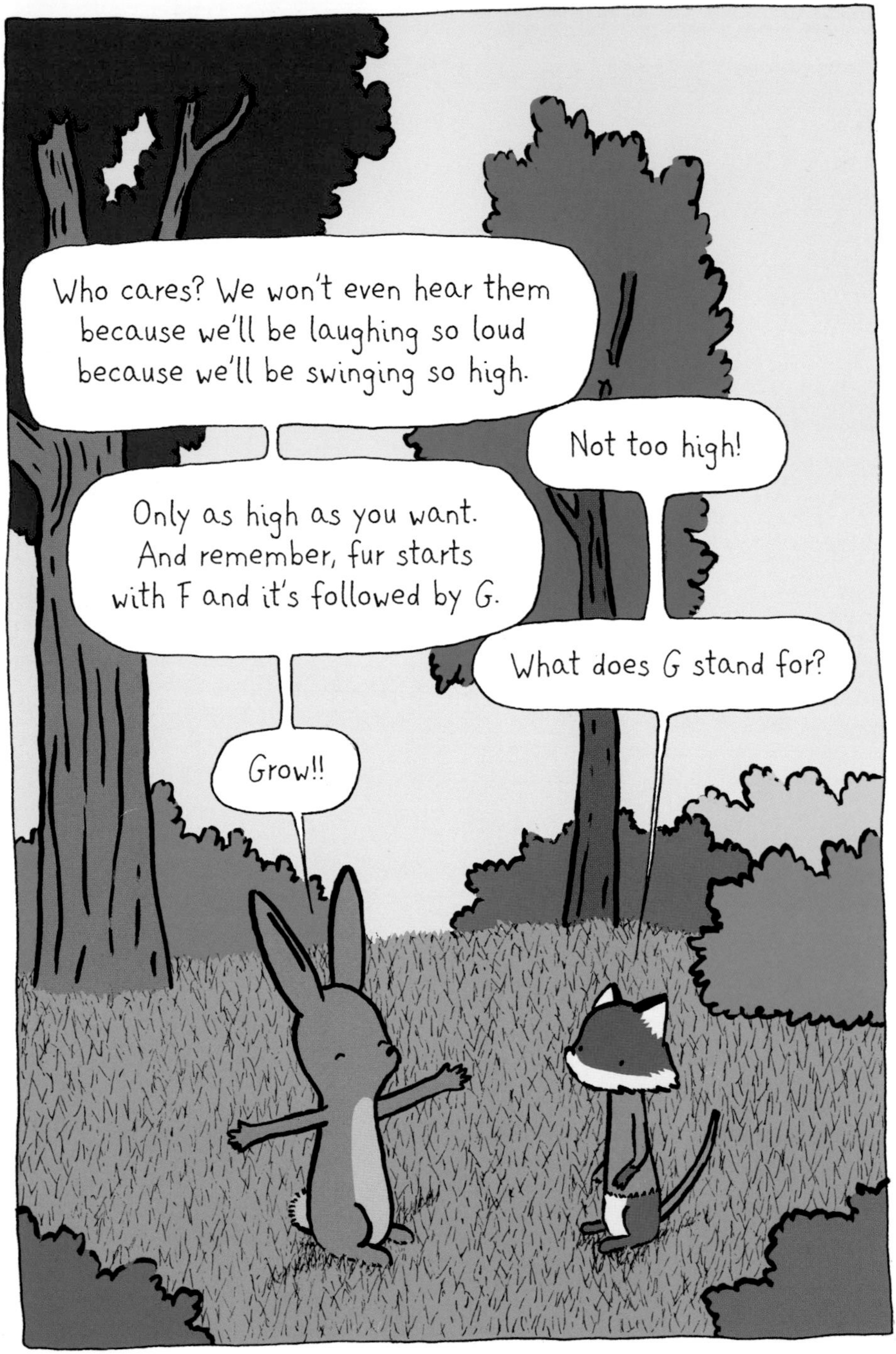
Who cares? We won't even hear them because we'll be laughing so loud because we'll be swinging so high.
Only as high as you want. And remember, fur starts with F and it's followed by G.
Not too high!
What does G stand for?
Grow!!

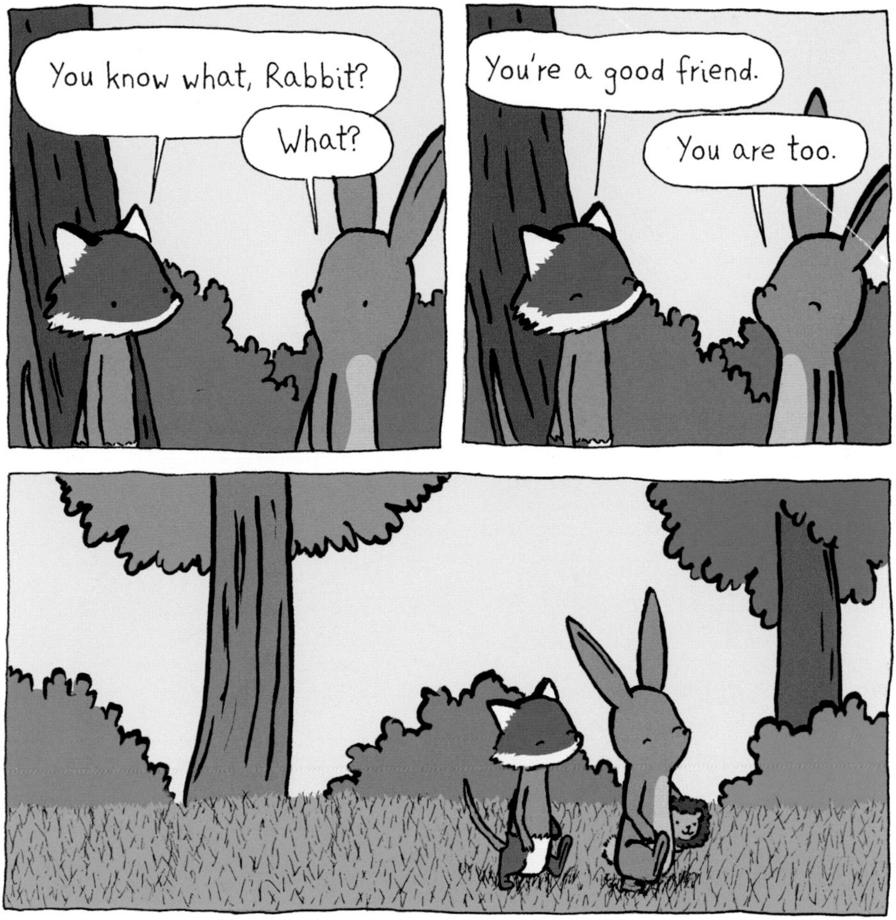
You know what, Rabbit?
What?
You're a good friend.
You are too.

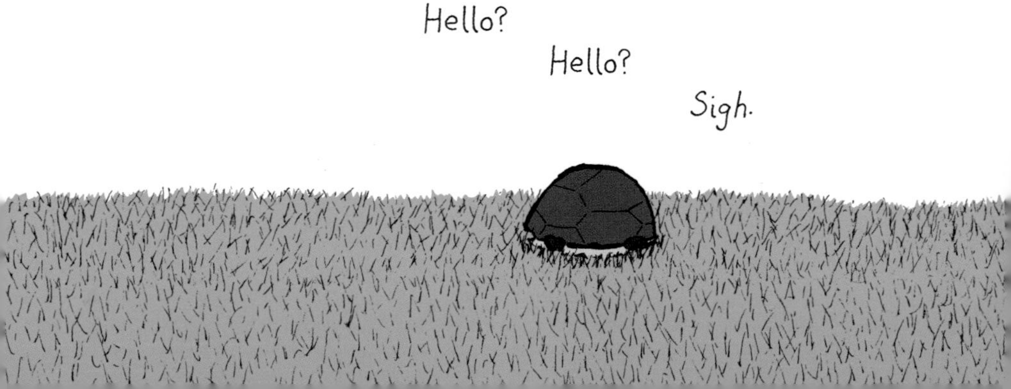
Hello?
Hello?
Sigh.

SWINGS, WINGS & SCARY THINGS

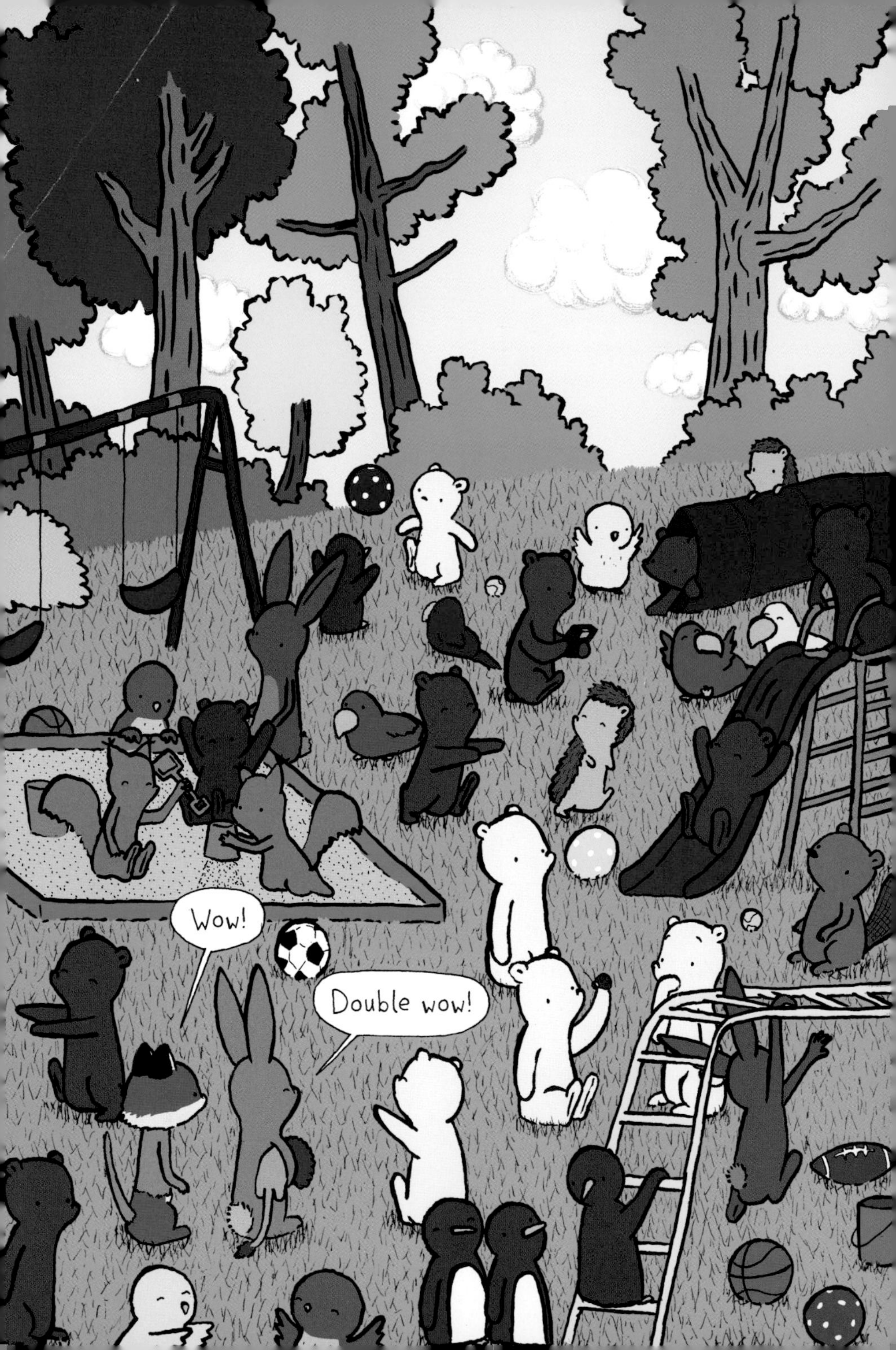
Wow!
Double wow!

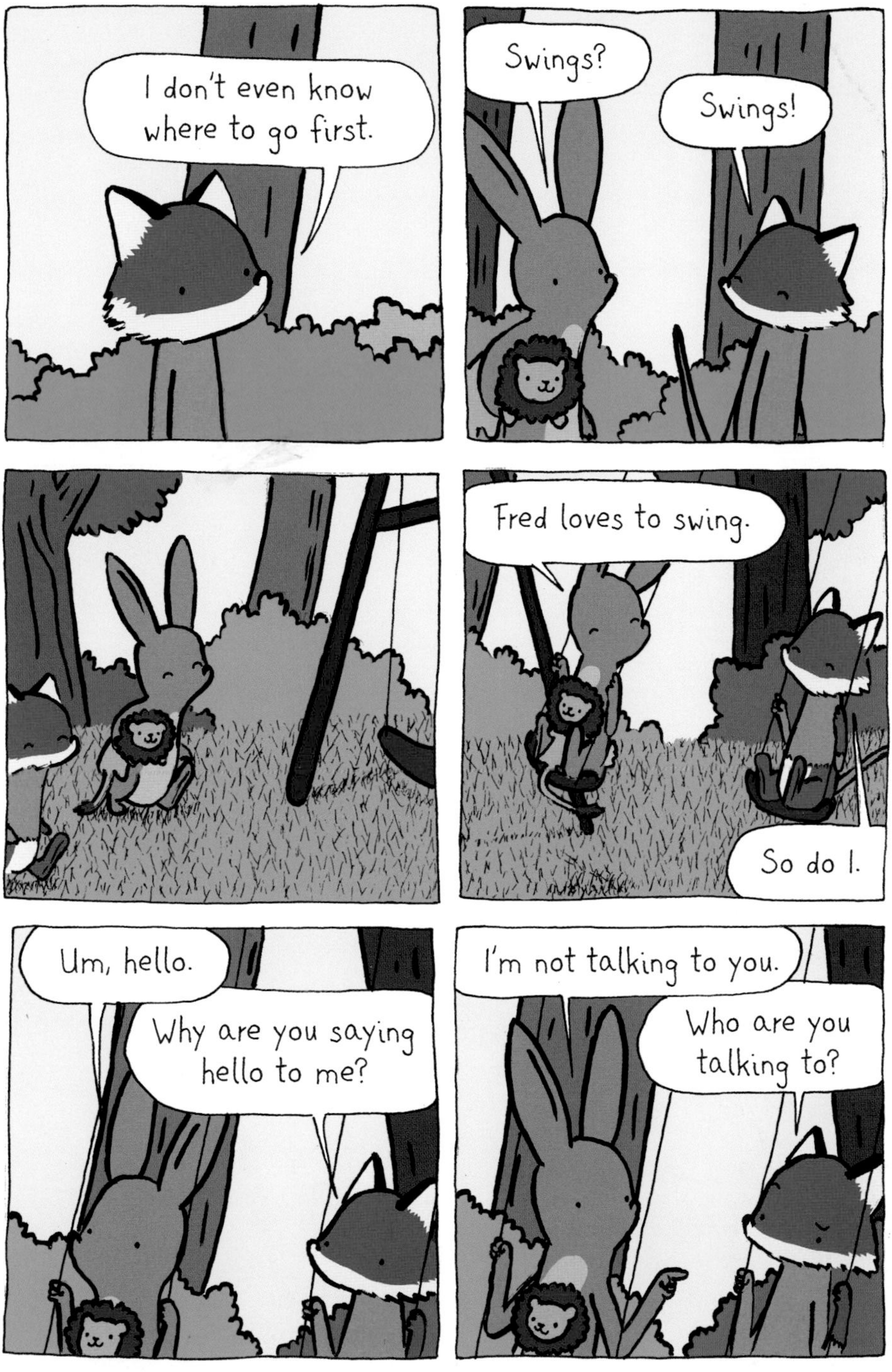
I don't even know where to go first.
Swings?
Swings!
Fred loves to swing.
So do I.
Um, hello.
Why are you saying hello to me?
I'm not talking to you.
Who are you talking to?

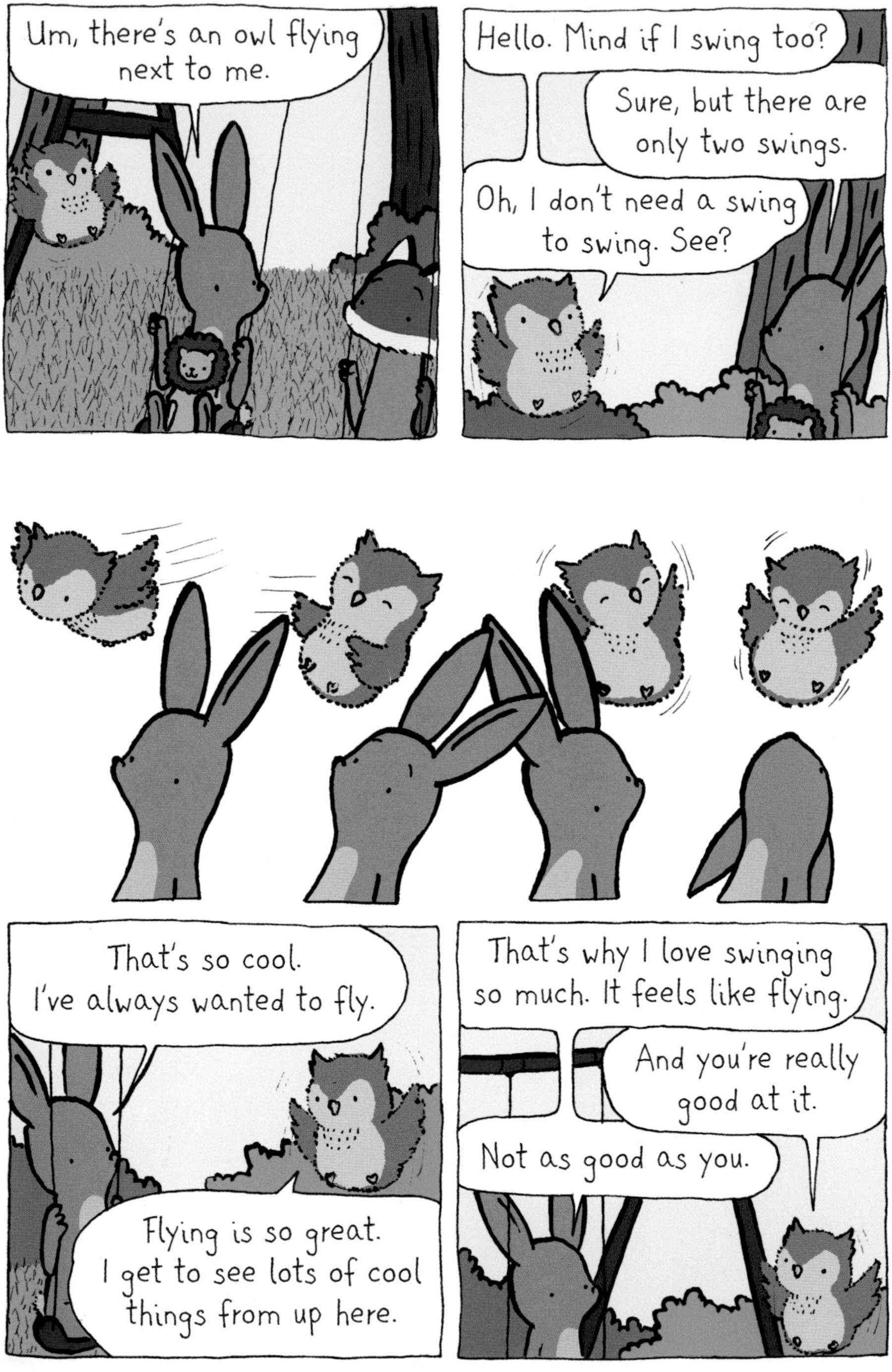
Um, there's an owl flying next to me.
Hello. Mind if I swing too?
Sure, but there are only two swings.
Oh, I don't need a swing to swing. See?
That's so cool. I've always wanted to fly.
Flying is so great. I get to see lots of cool things from up here.
That's why I love swinging so much. It feels like flying.
And you're really good at it.
Not as good as you.

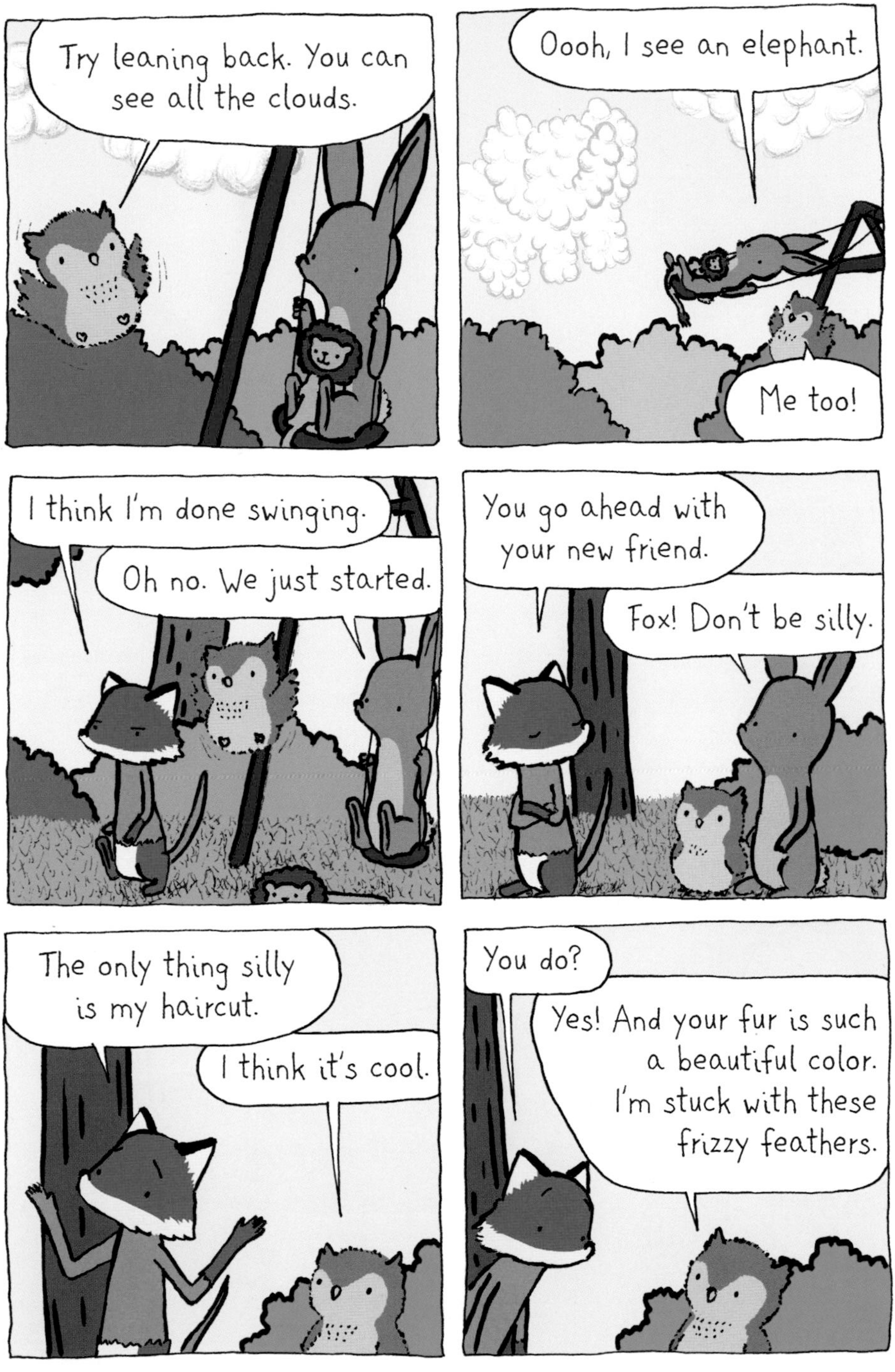
Try leaning back. You can see all the clouds.
Oooh, I see an elephant.
Me too!
I think I'm done swinging.
Oh no. We just started.
You go ahead with your new friend.
Fox! Don't be silly.
The only thing silly is my haircut.
I think it's cool.
You do?
Yes! And your fur is such a beautiful color. I'm stuck with these frizzy feathers.

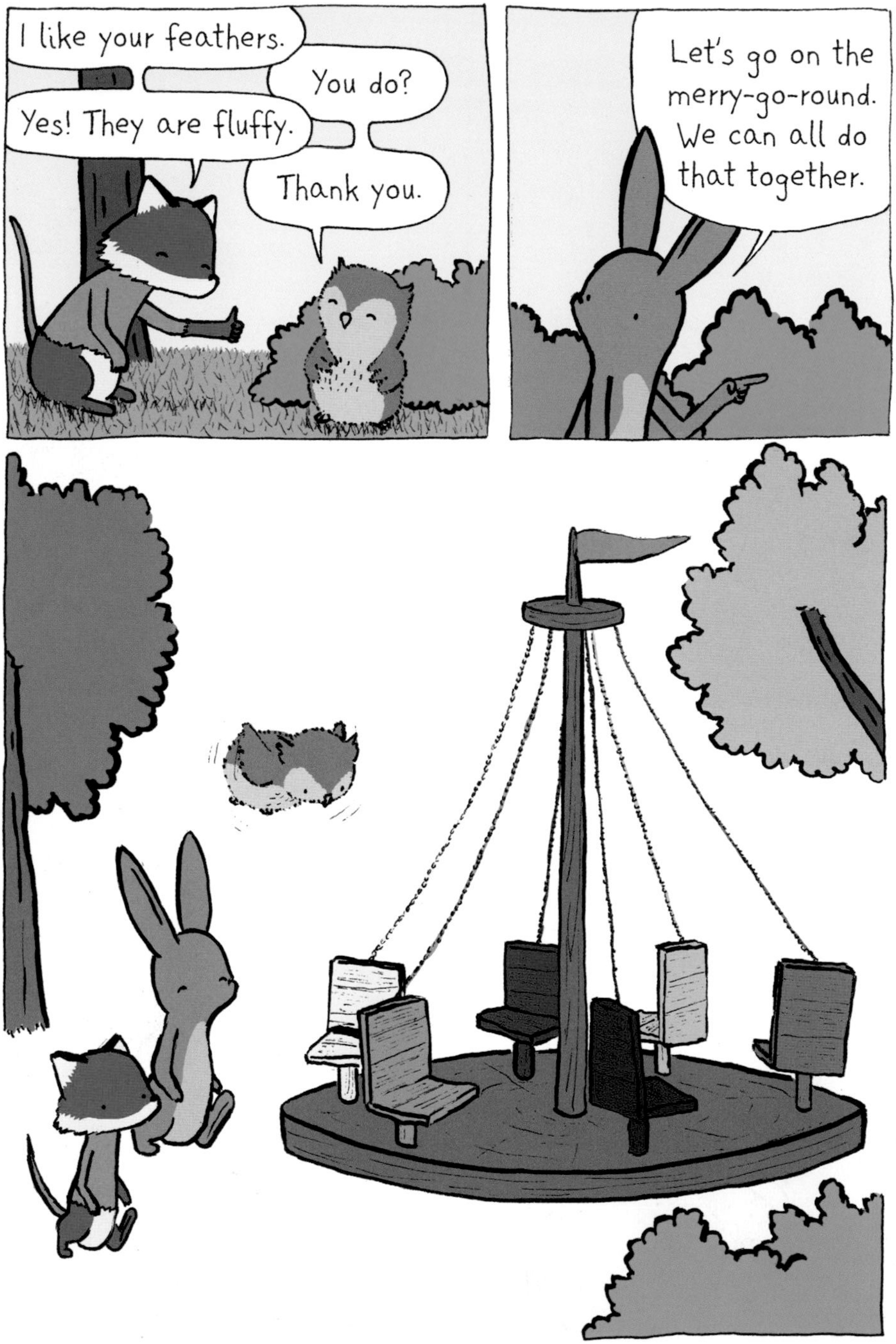
I like your feathers.
You do?
Yes! They are fluffy.
Thank you.
Let's go on the merry-go-round. We can all do that together.

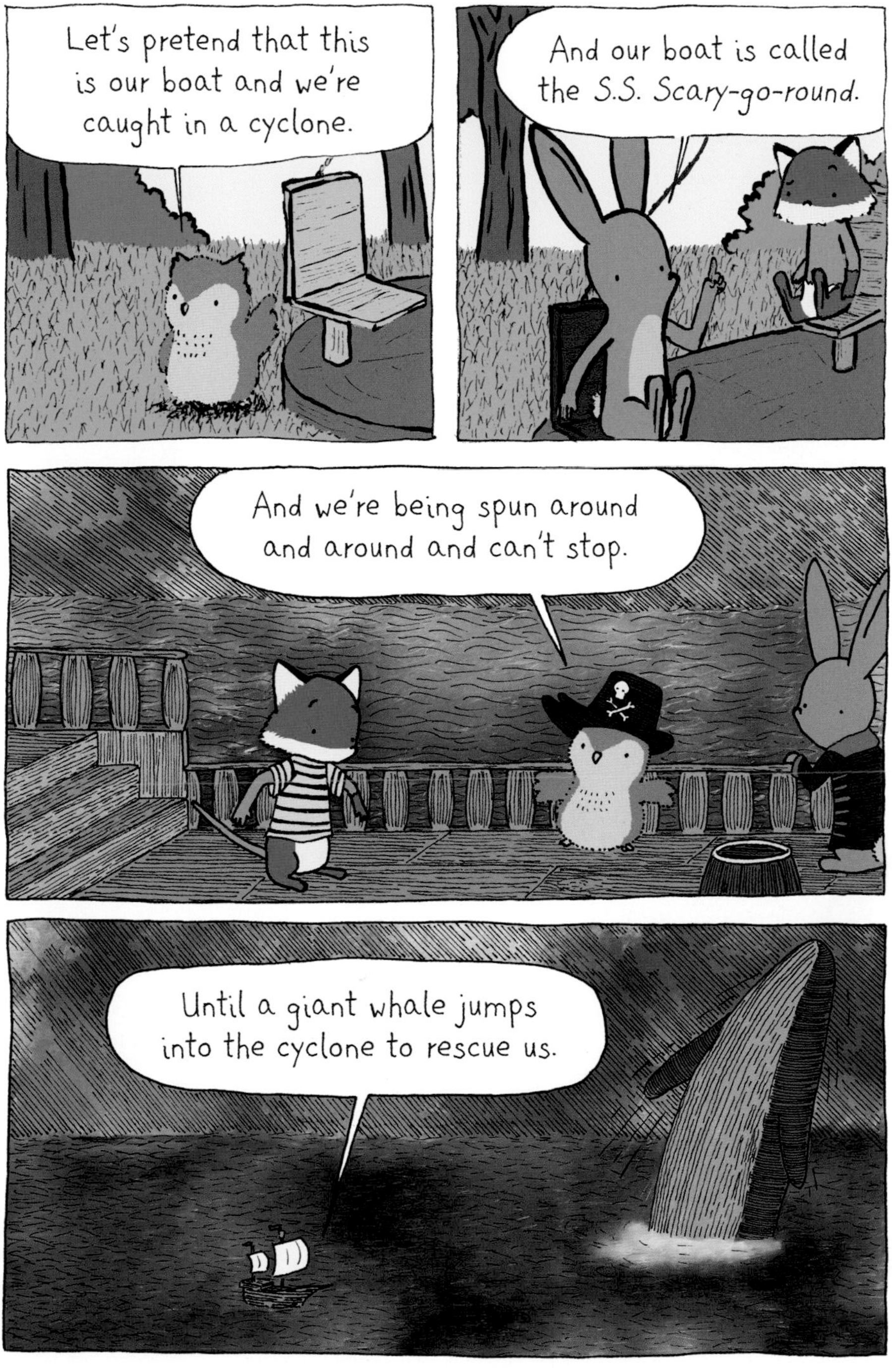
Let's pretend that this is our boat and we're caught in a cyclone.
And our boat is called the *S.S. Scary-go-round.*
And we're being spun around and around and can't stop.
Until a giant whale jumps into the cyclone to rescue us.

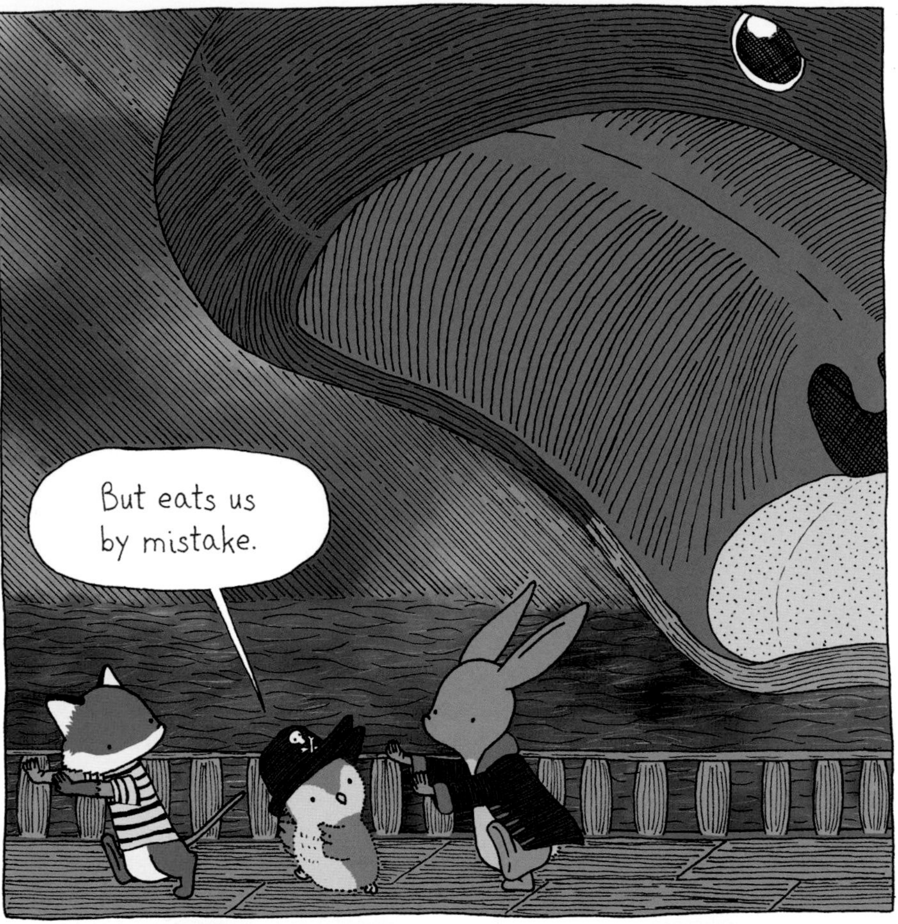
But eats us by mistake.

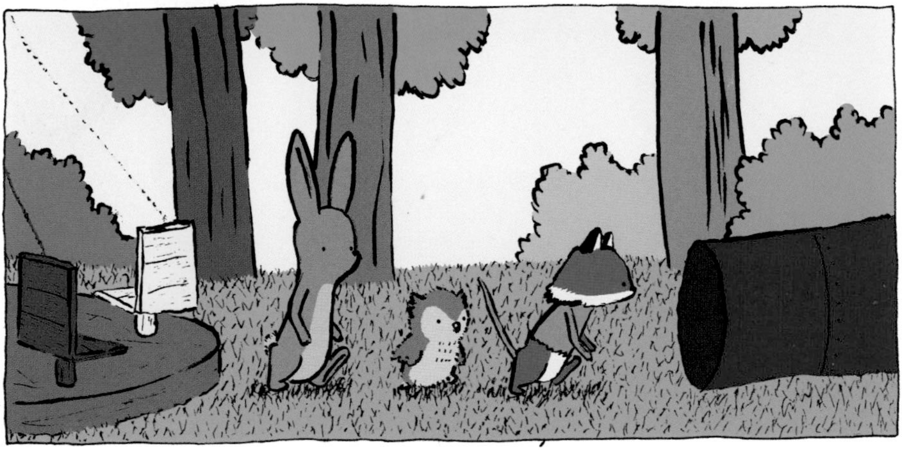

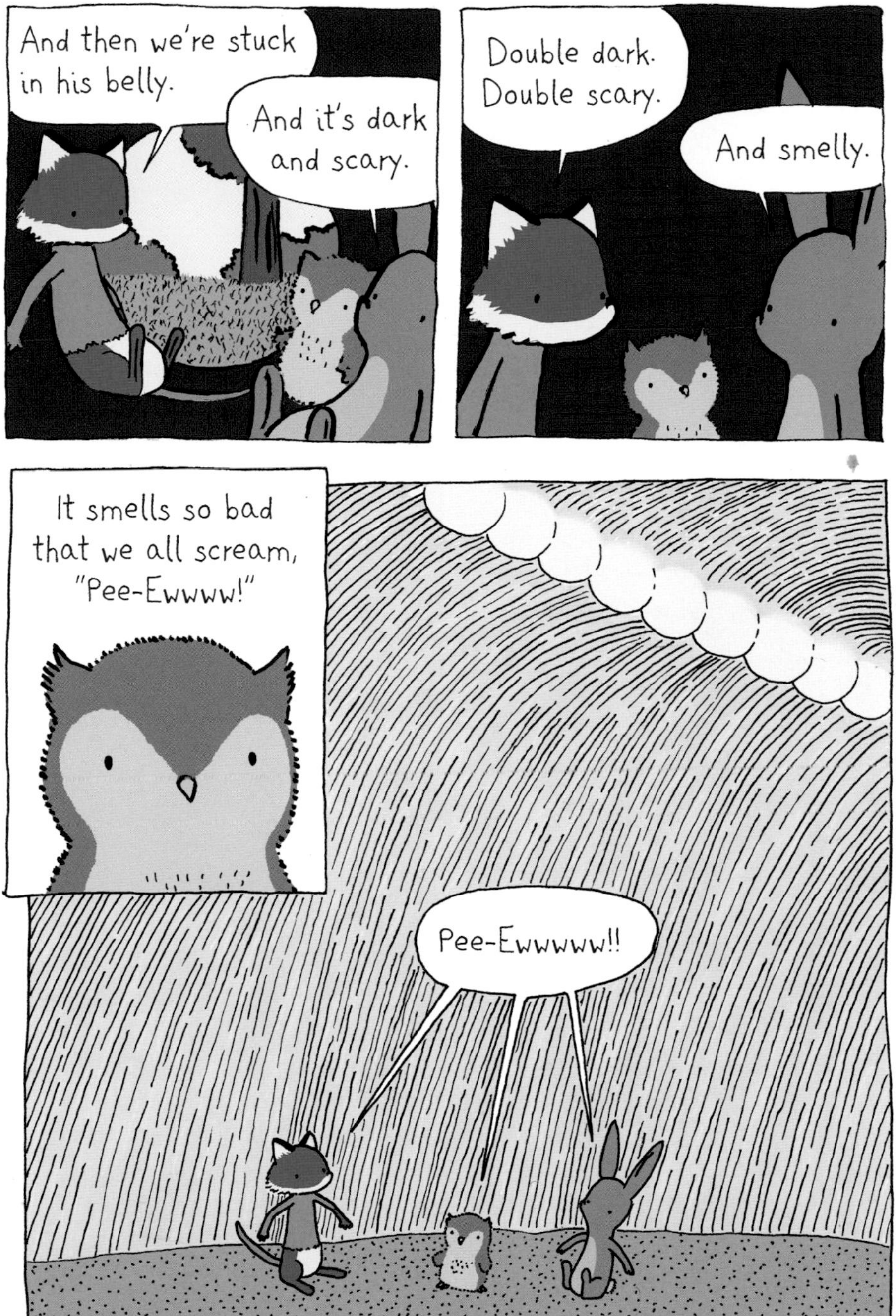
And then we're stuck in his belly.
And it's dark and scary.
Double dark. Double scary.
And smelly.
It smells so bad that we all scream, "Pee-Ewwww!"
Pee-Ewwwww!!

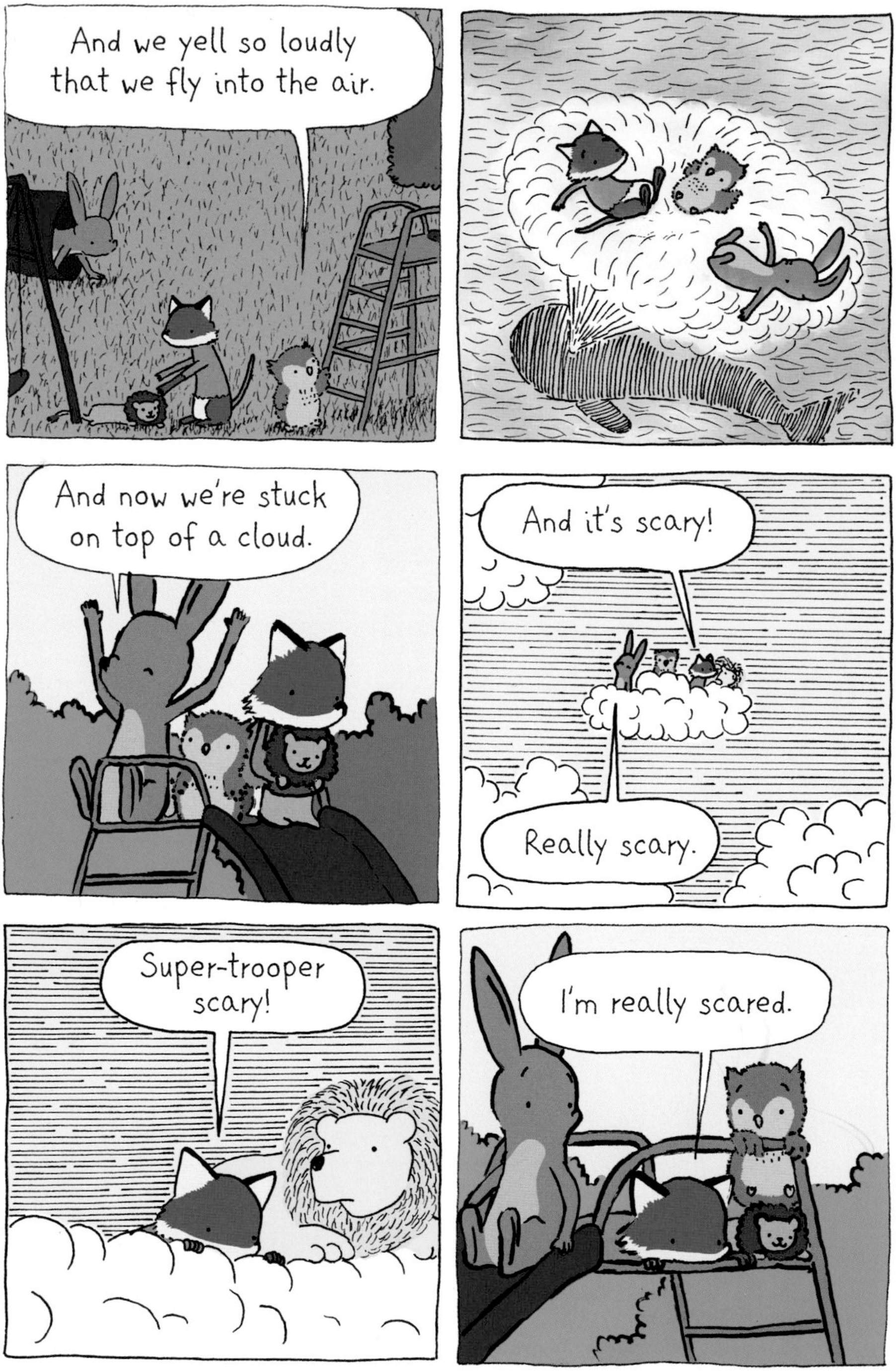
And we yell so loudly that we fly into the air.
And now we're stuck on top of a cloud.
And it's scary!
Really scary.
Super-trooper scary!
I'm really scared.

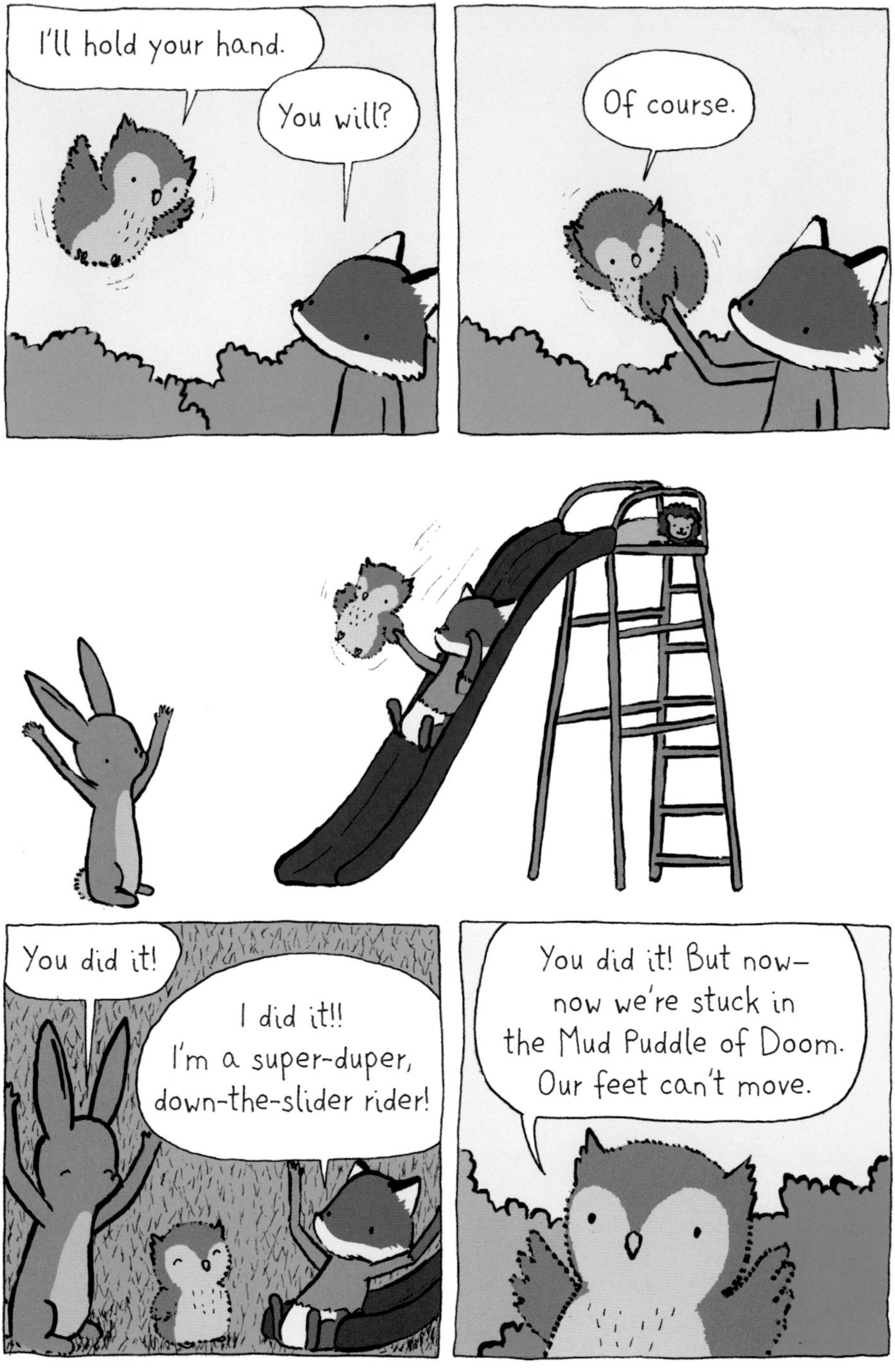
I'll hold your hand.
You will?
Of course.
You did it!
I did it!! I'm a super-duper, down-the-slider rider!
You did it! But now—now we're stuck in the Mud Puddle of Doom. Our feet can't move.

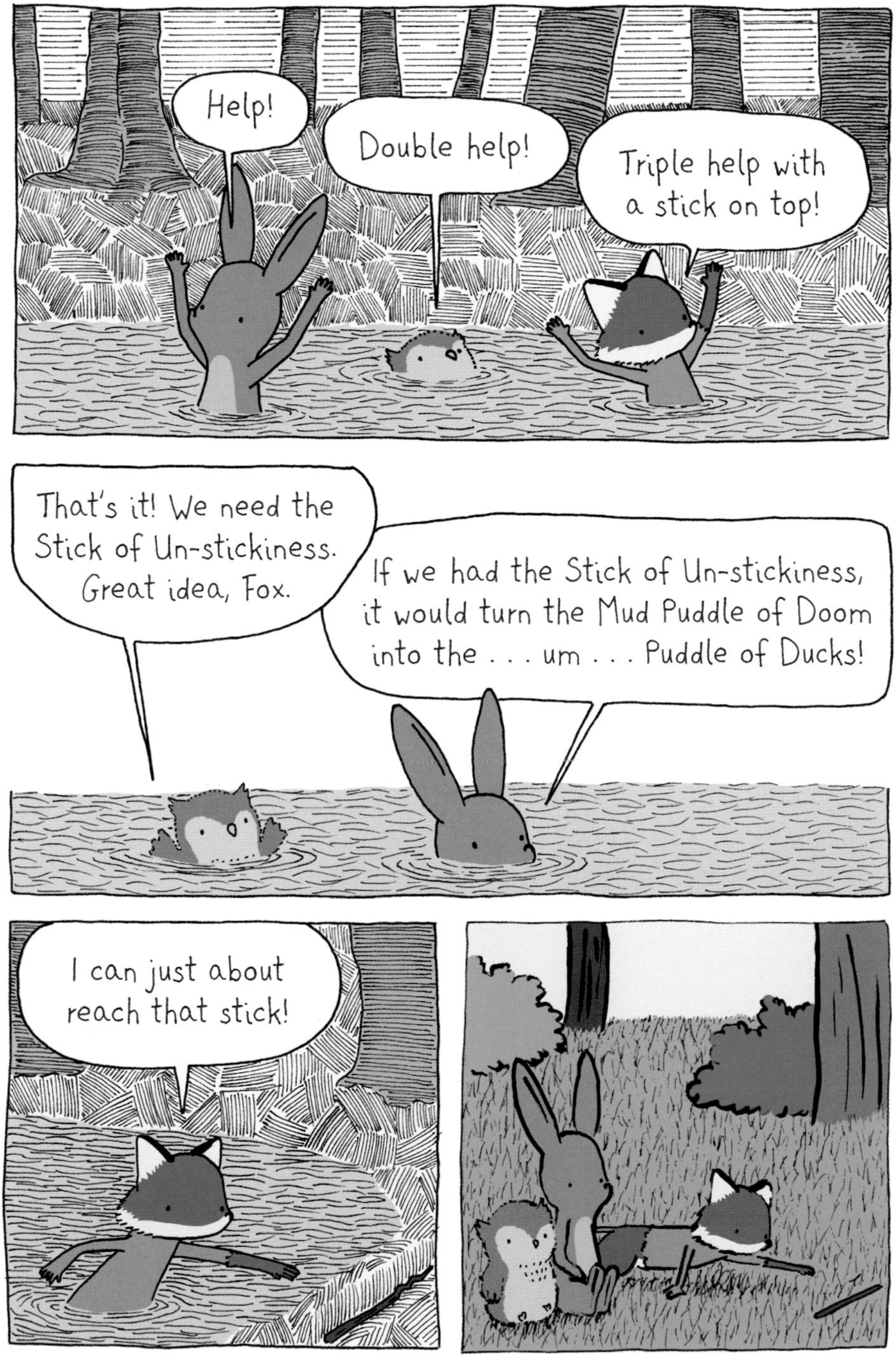
Help!
Double help!
Triple help with a stick on top!
That's it! We need the Stick of Un-stickiness. Great idea, Fox.
If we had the Stick of Un-stickiness, it would turn the Mud Puddle of Doom into the . . . um . . . Puddle of Ducks!
I can just about reach that stick!

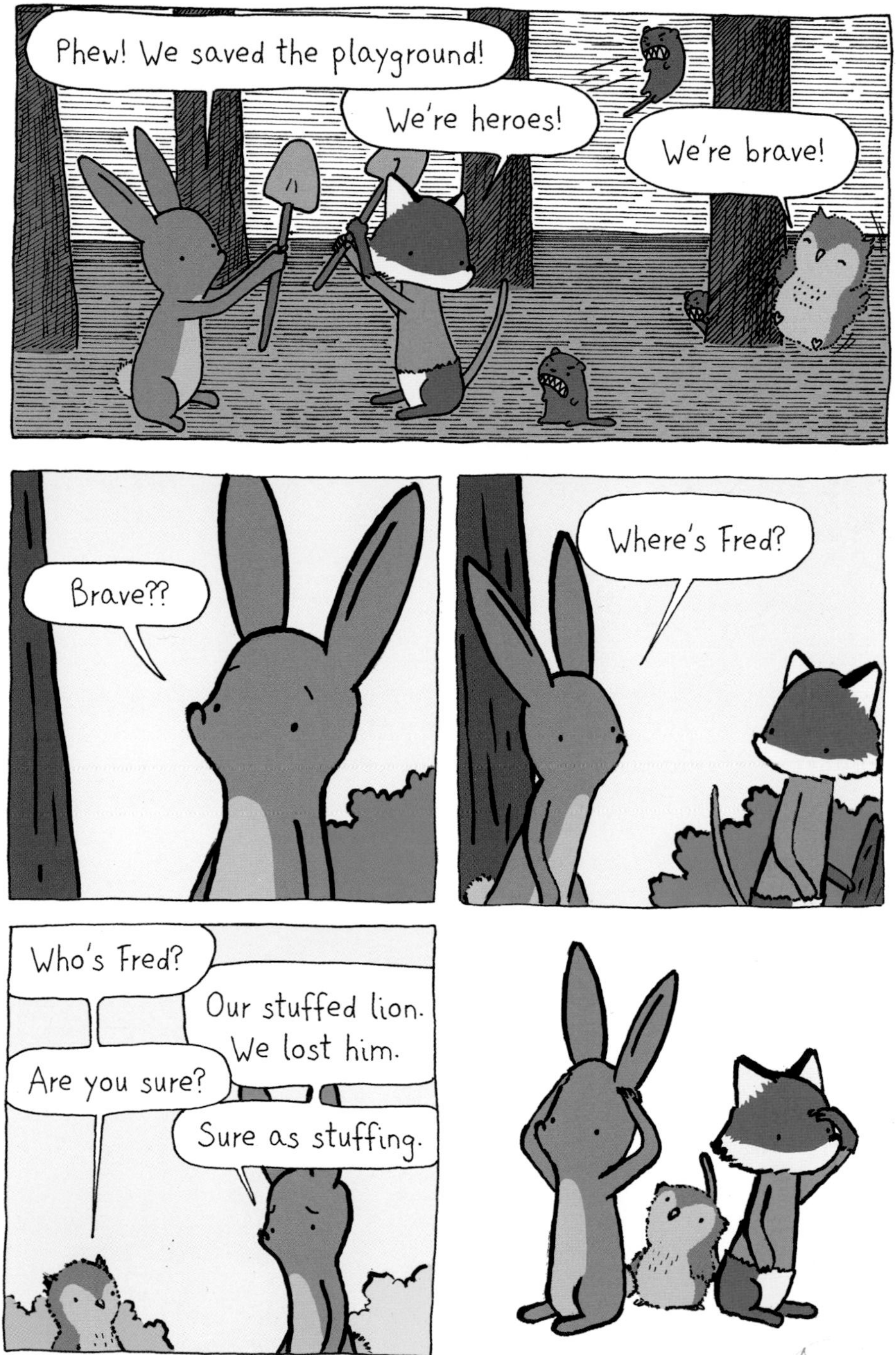
Phew! We saved the playground!
We're heroes!
We're brave!
Brave??
Where's Fred?
Who's Fred?
Our stuffed lion. We lost him.
Are you sure?
Sure as stuffing.

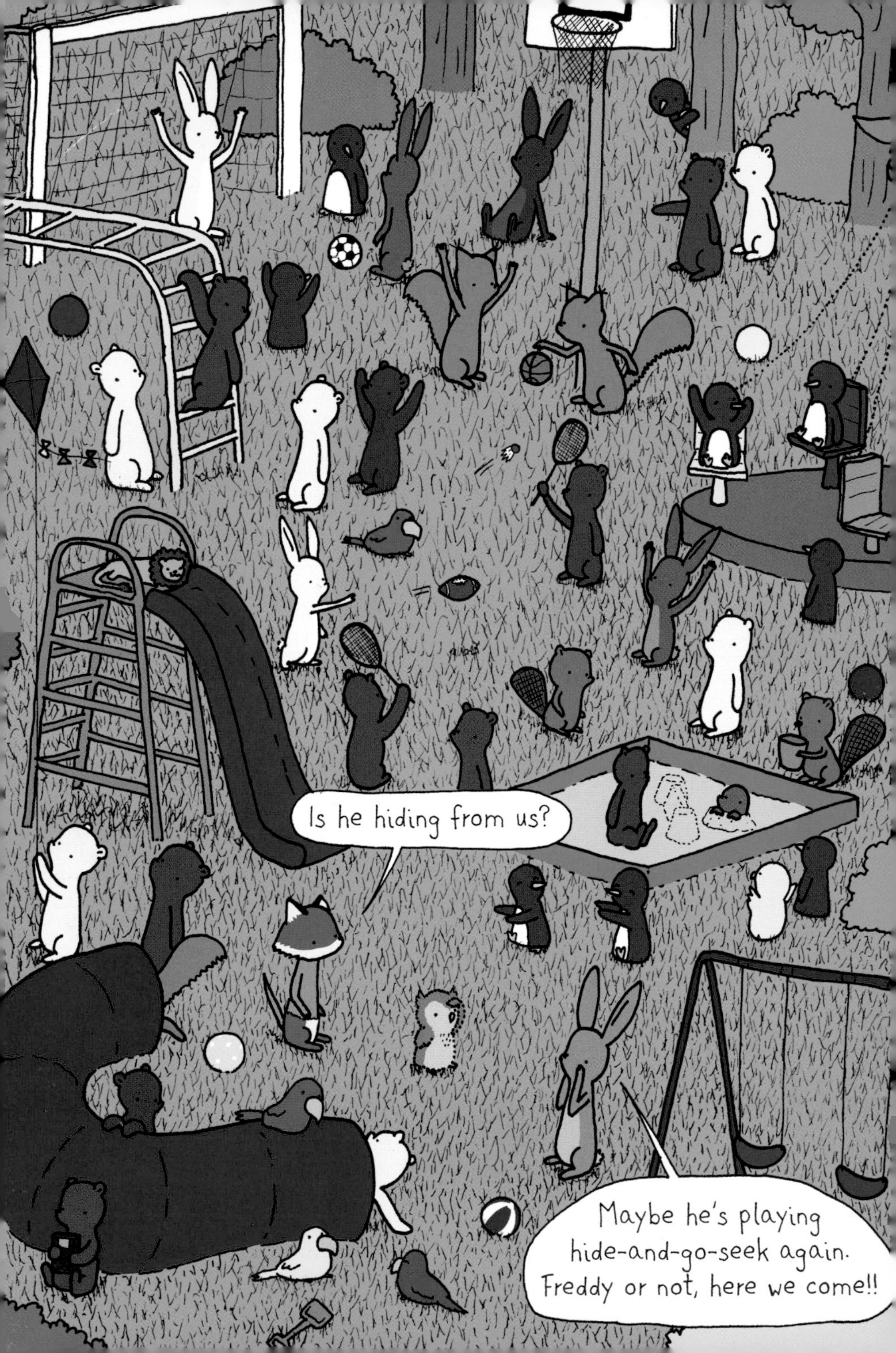

Is he hiding from us?
Maybe he's playing hide-and-go-seek again. Freddy or not, here we come!!

48

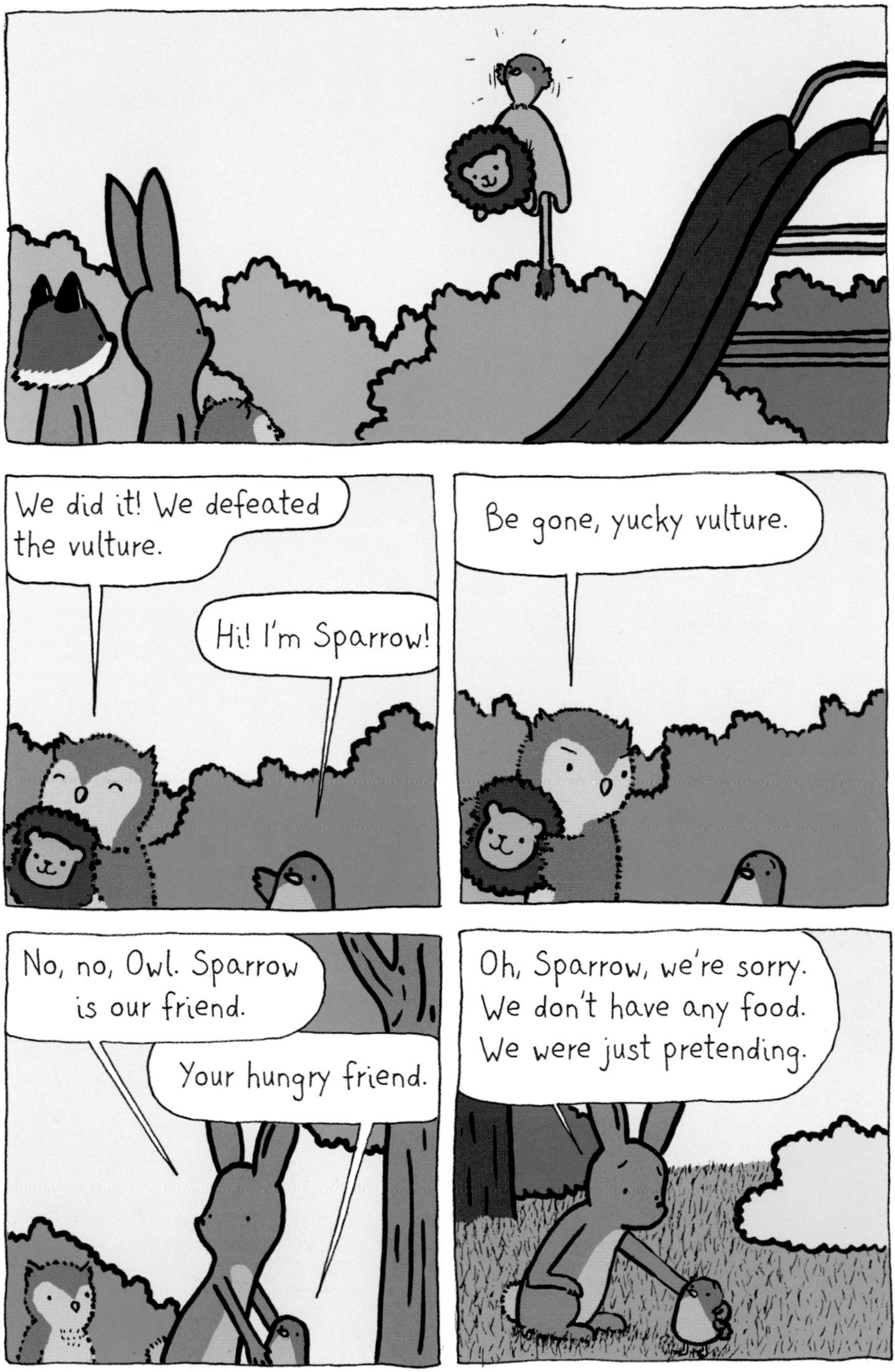
We did it! We defeated the vulture.
Hi! I'm Sparrow!
Be gone, yucky vulture.
No, no, Owl. Sparrow is our friend.
Your hungry friend.
Oh, Sparrow, we're sorry. We don't have any food. We were just pretending.

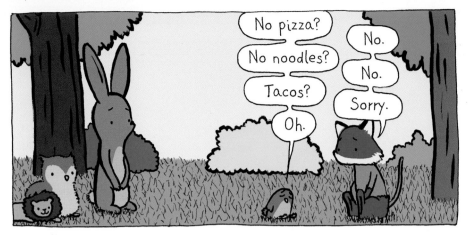

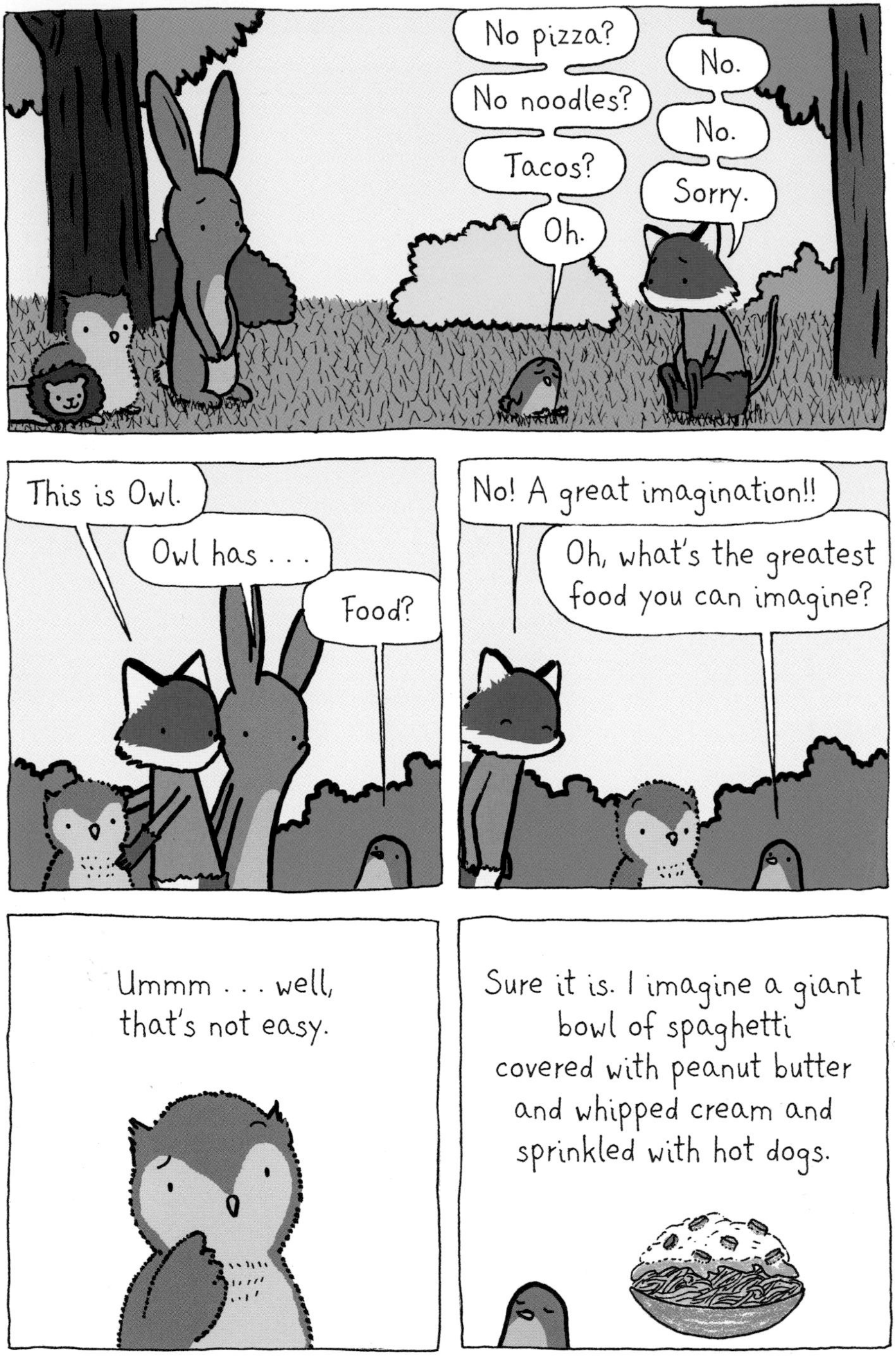
No pizza?
No.
No noodles?
No.
Tacos?
Sorry.
Oh.
This is Owl.
Owl has . . .
Food?
No! A great imagination!!
Oh, what's the greatest food you can imagine?
Ummm . . . well, that's not easy.
Sure it is. I imagine a giant bowl of spaghetti covered with peanut butter and whipped cream and sprinkled with hot dogs.

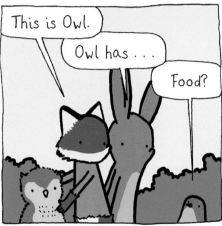

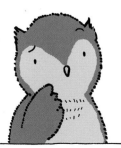

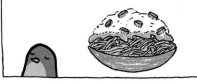

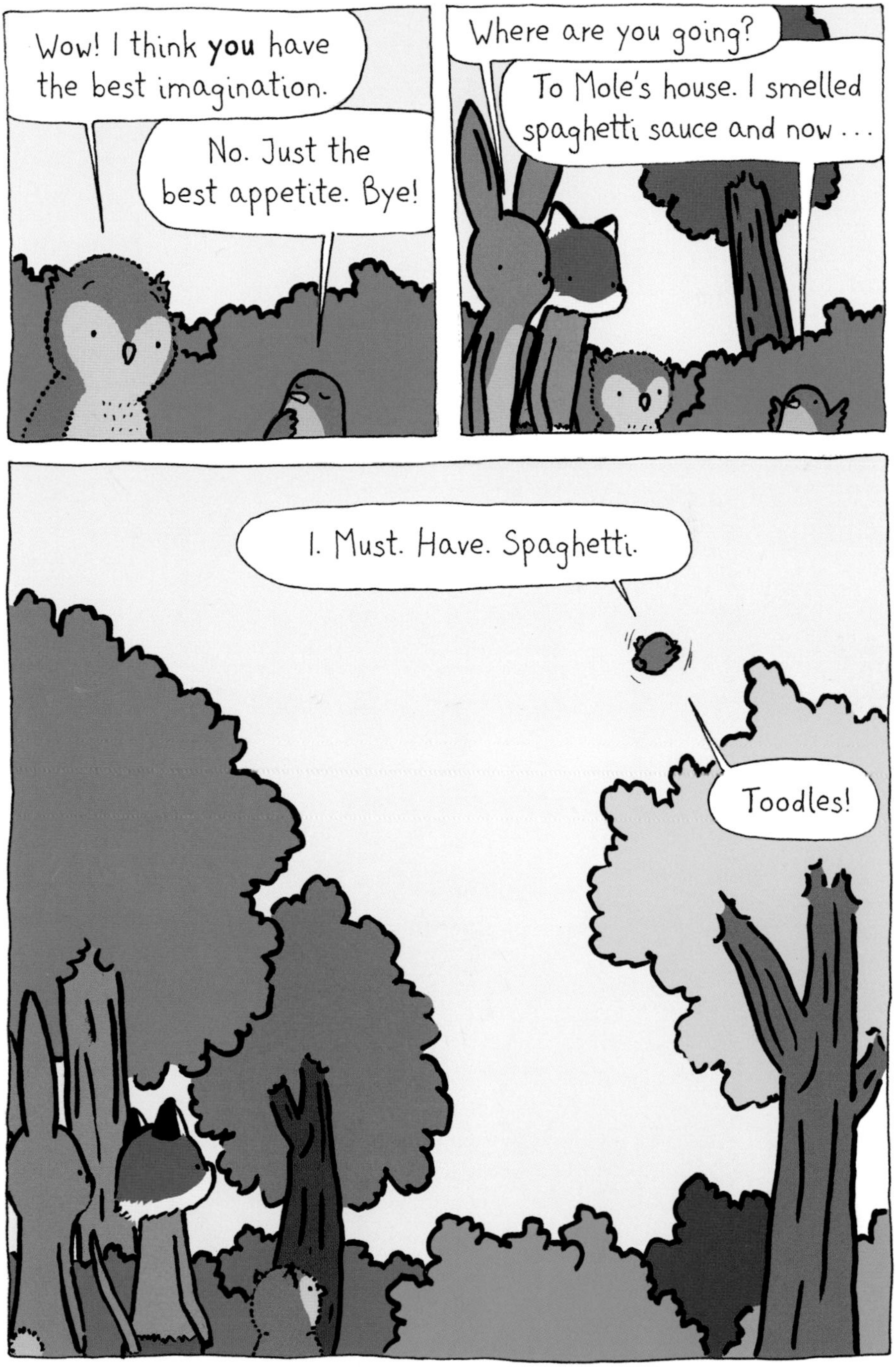
Wow! I think **you** have the best imagination.
No. Just the best appetite. Bye!
Where are you going?
To Mole's house. I smelled spaghetti sauce and now . . .
I. Must. Have. Spaghetti.
Toodles!

STORY FOUR

FALL, FARM & FINICKY

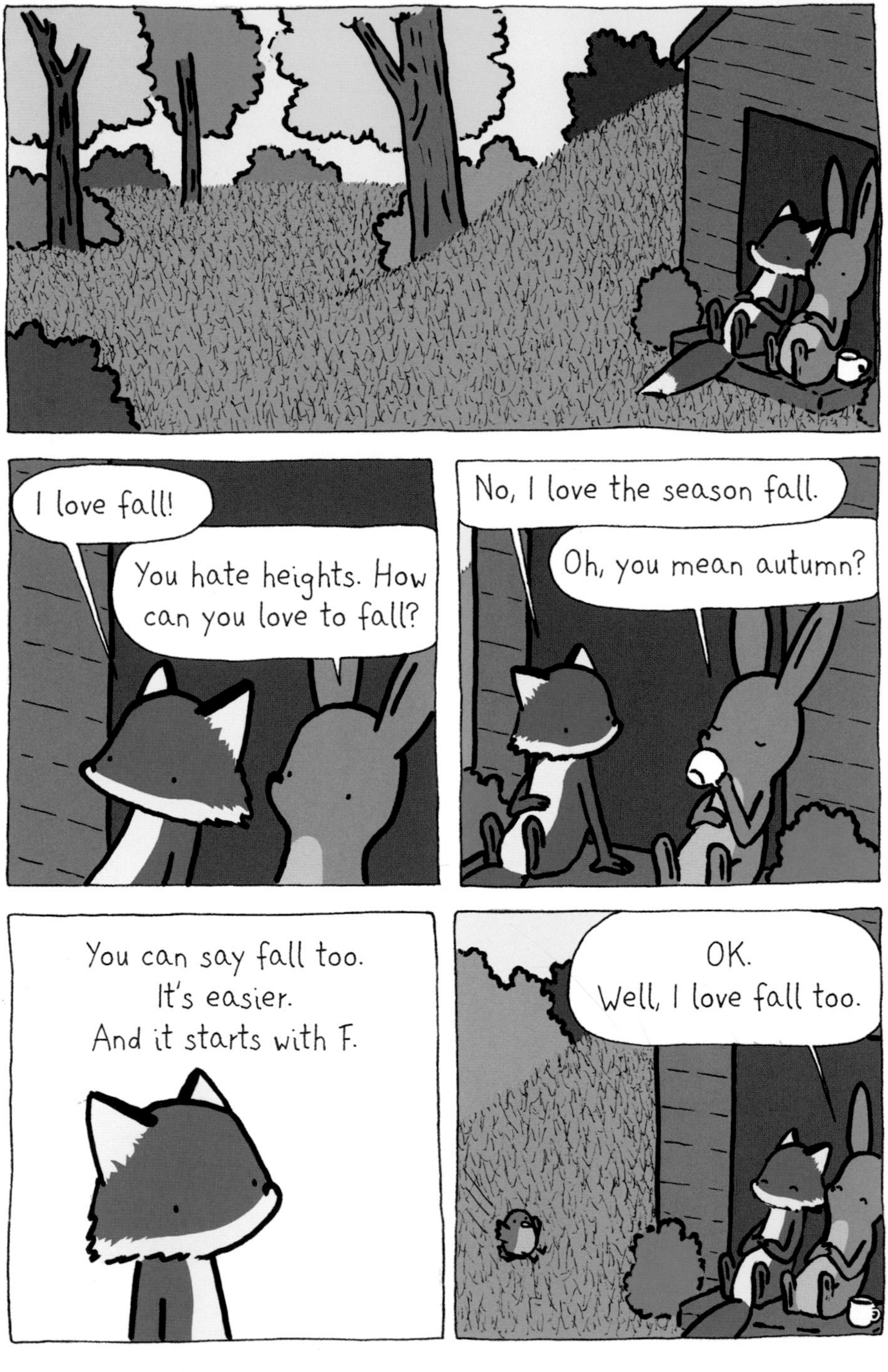
I love fall!
You hate heights. How can you love to fall?
No, I love the season fall.
Oh, you mean autumn?
You can say fall too. It's easier. And it starts with F.
OK. Well, I love fall too.

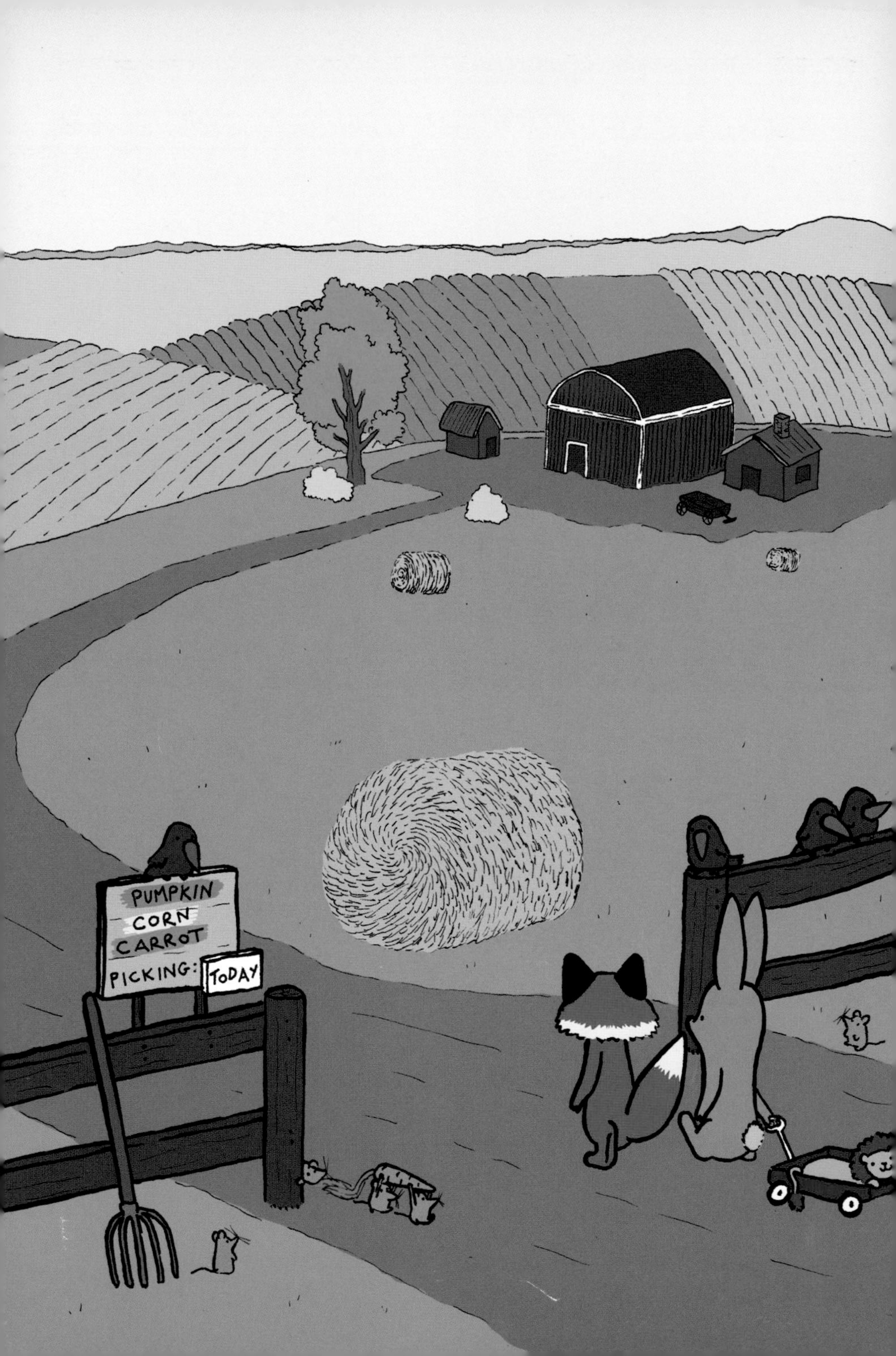
PUMPKIN
CORN
CARROT
PICKING: TODAY

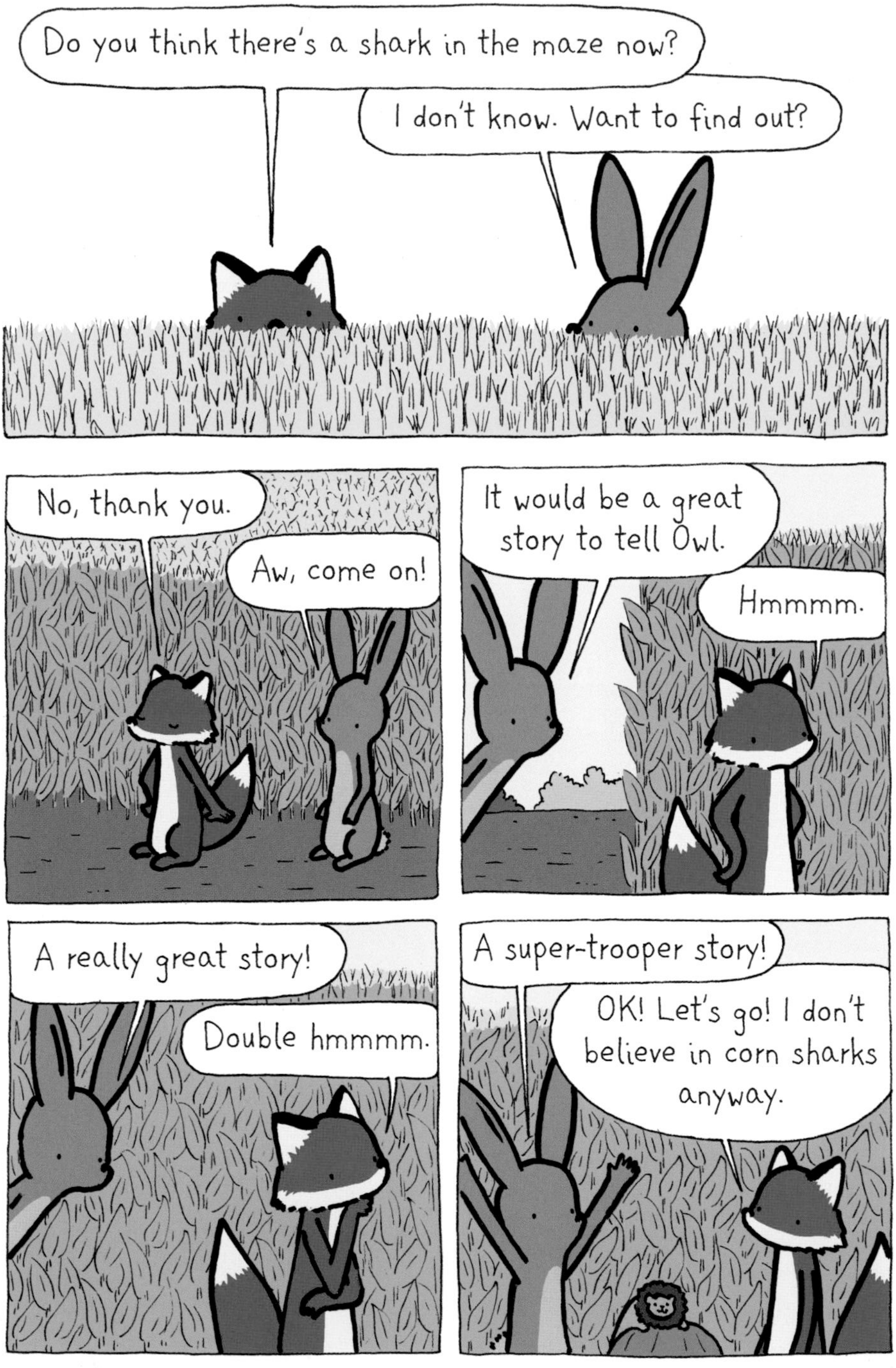
Do you think there's a shark in the maze now?
I don't know. Want to find out?
No, thank you.
Aw, come on!
It would be a great story to tell Owl.
Hmmmm.
A really great story!
Double hmmmm.
A super-trooper story!
OK! Let's go! I don't believe in corn sharks anyway.

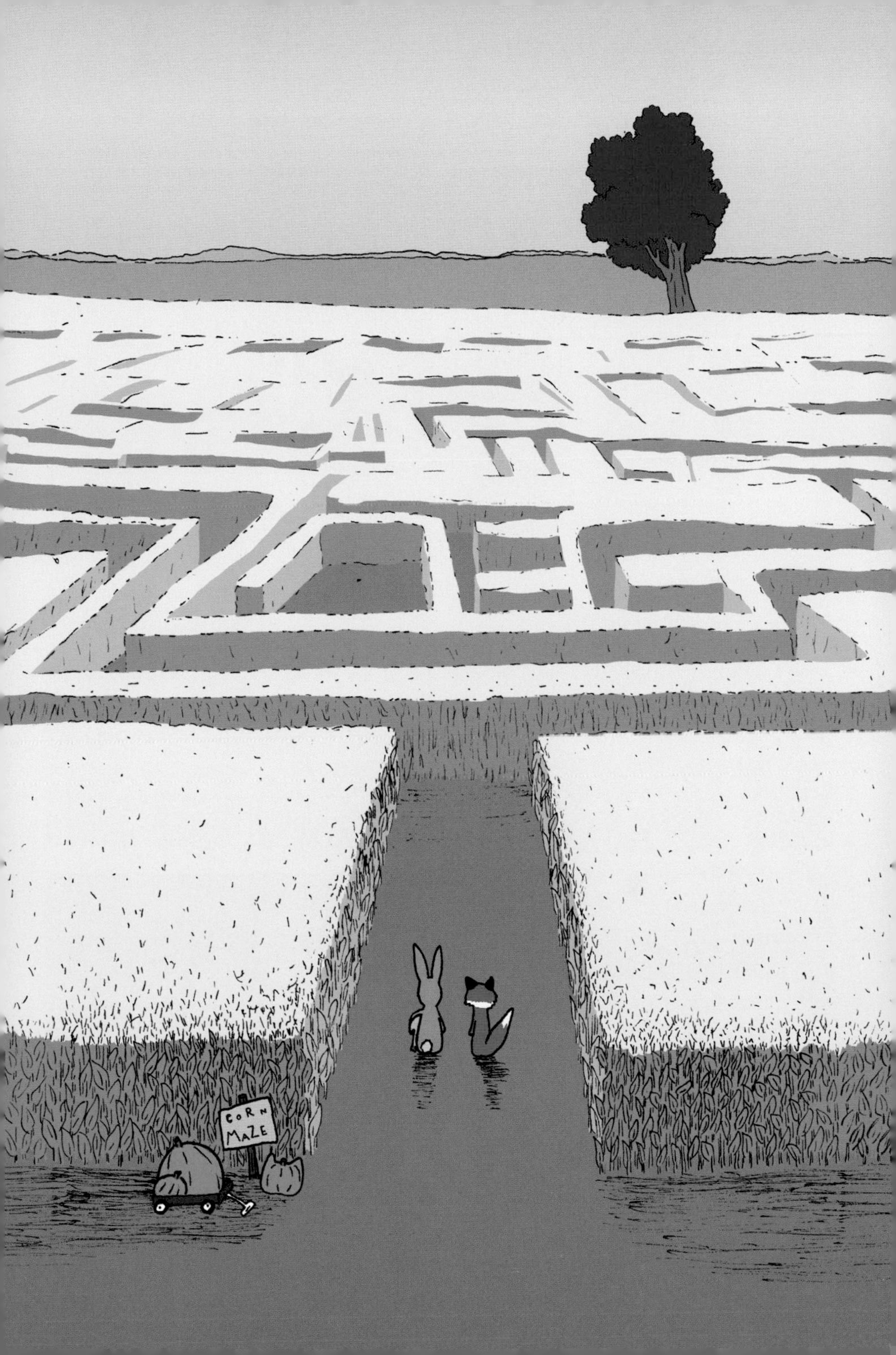
CORN MAZE

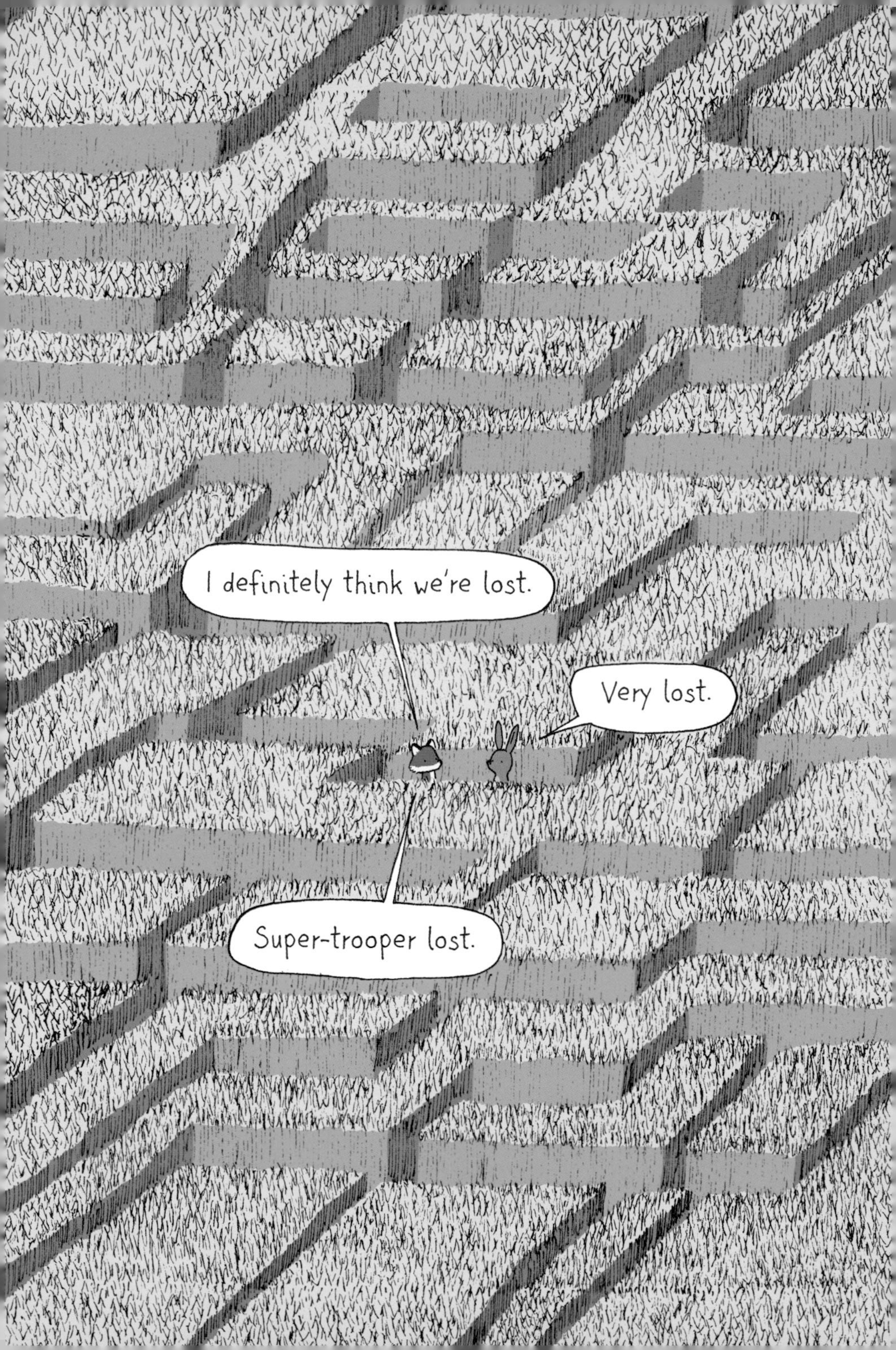
I definitely think we're lost.
Very lost.
Super-trooper lost.

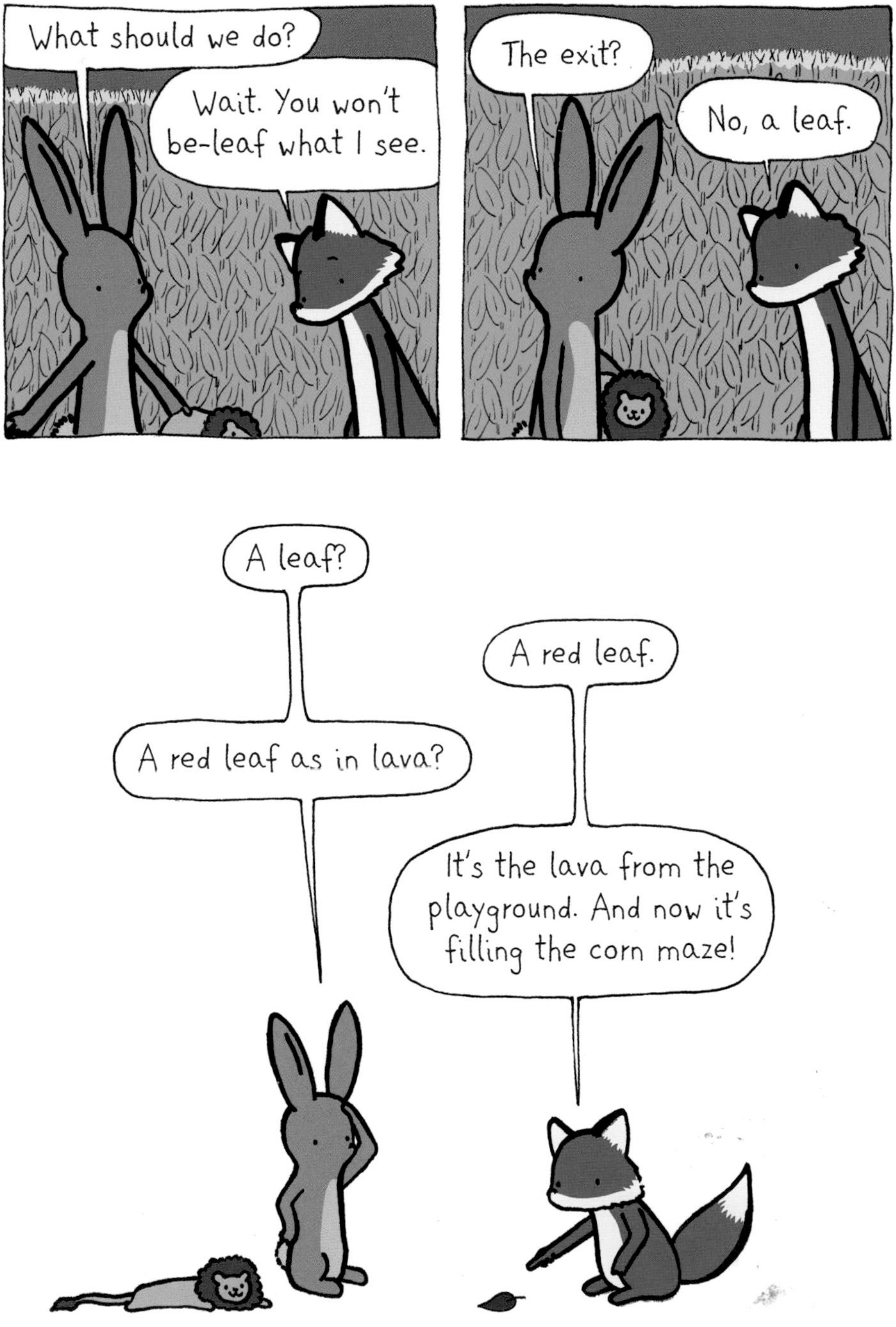
What should we do?
Wait. You won't be-leaf what I see.
The exit?
No, a leaf.
A leaf?
A red leaf.
A red leaf as in lava?
It's the lava from the playground. And now it's filling the corn maze!

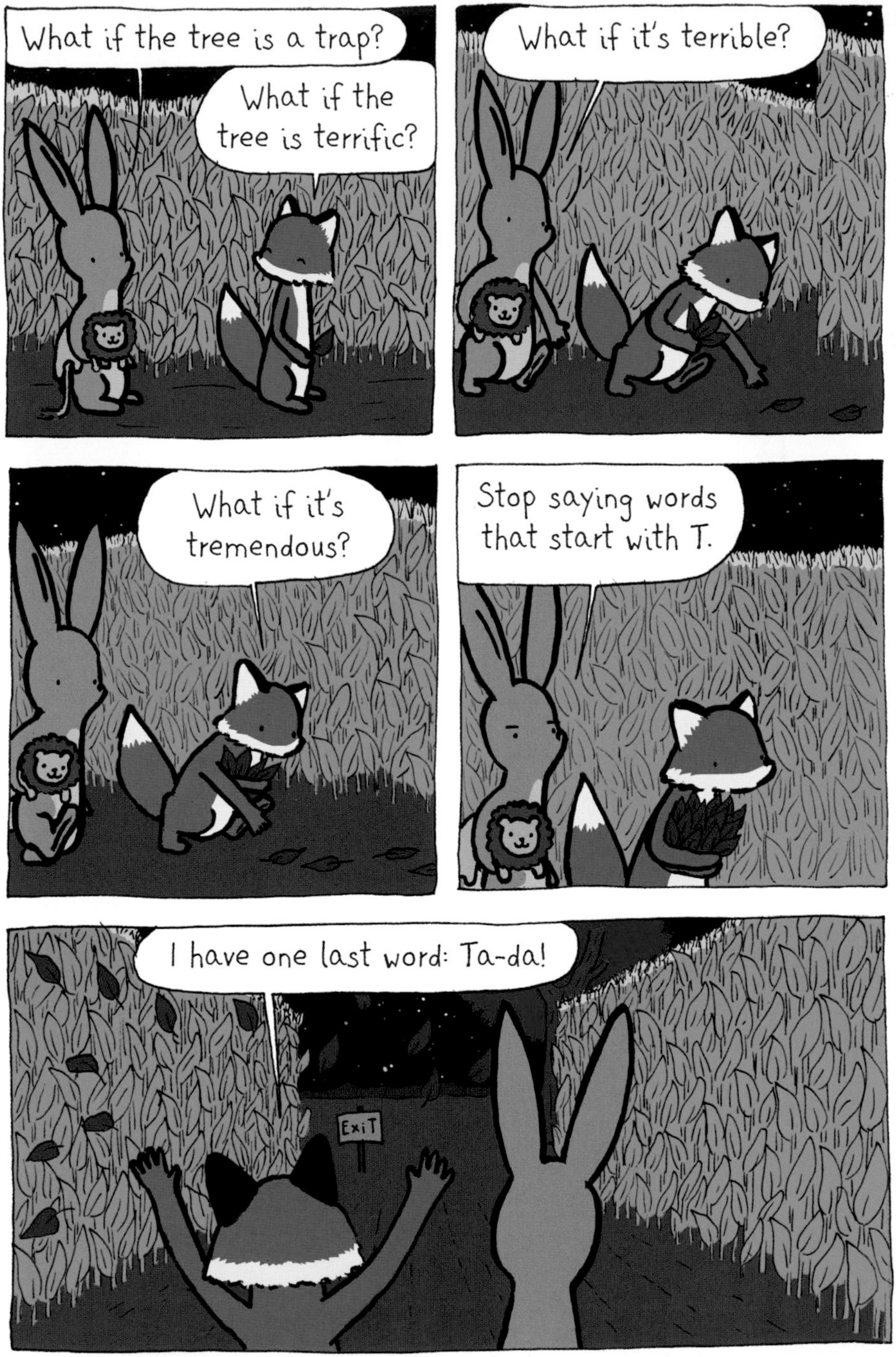
What if the tree is a trap?
What if the tree is terrific?
What if it's terrible?
What if it's tremendous?
Stop saying words that start with T.
I have one last word: Ta-da!
EXIT

STORY FIVE

FRIENDS & FIREFLIES

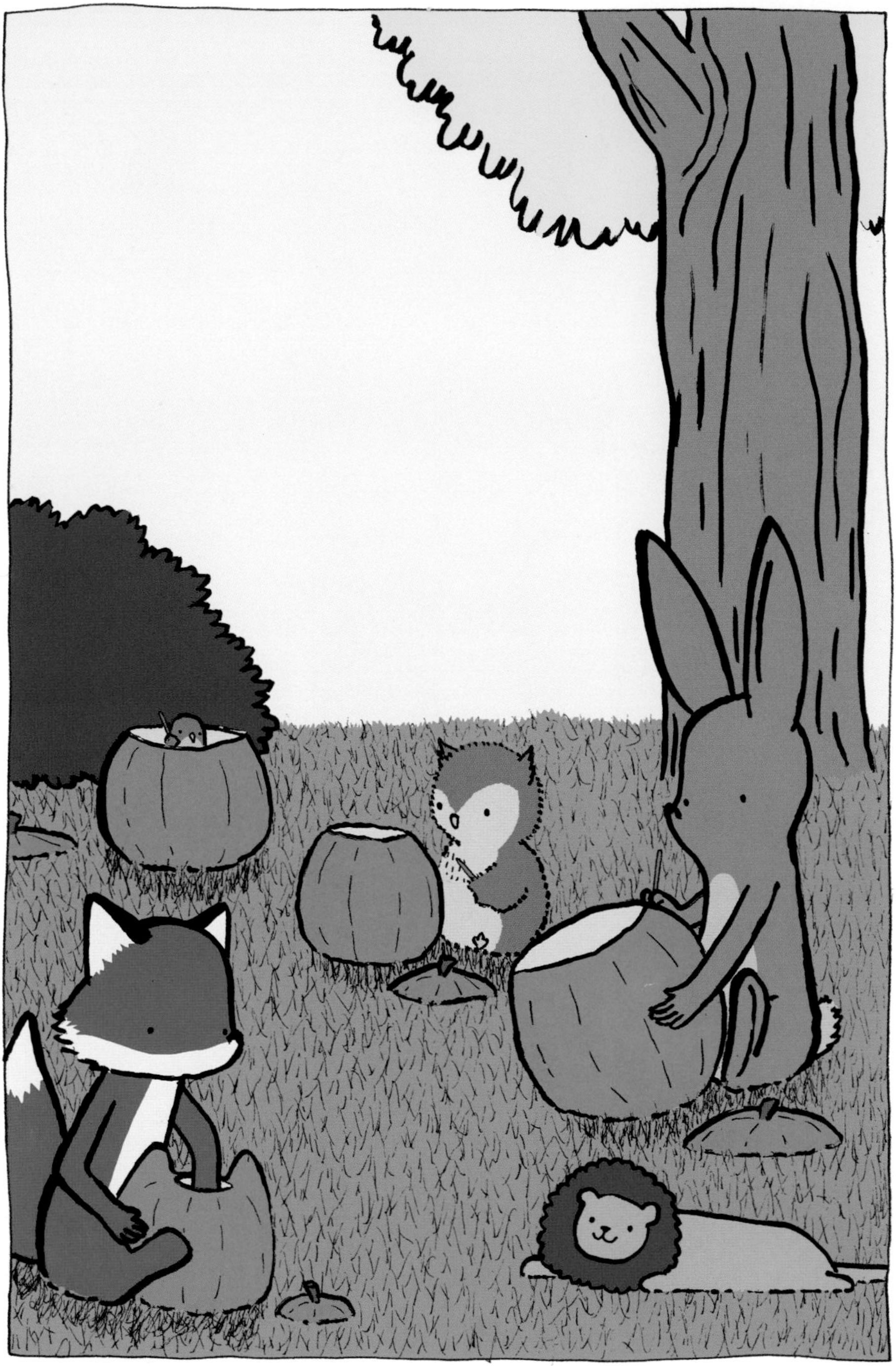

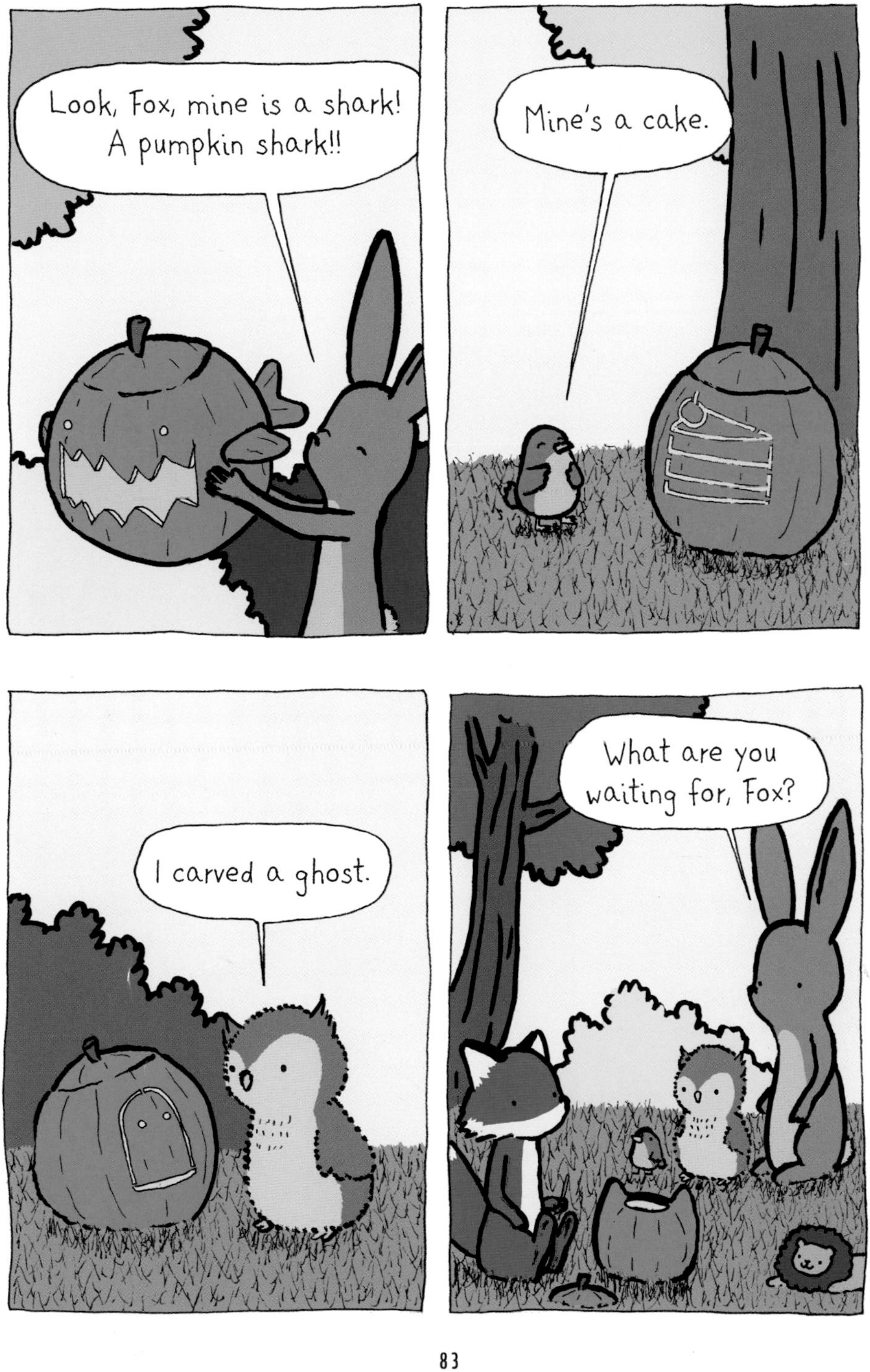
Look, Fox, mine is a shark! A pumpkin shark!!
Mine's a cake.
I carved a ghost.
What are you waiting for, Fox?

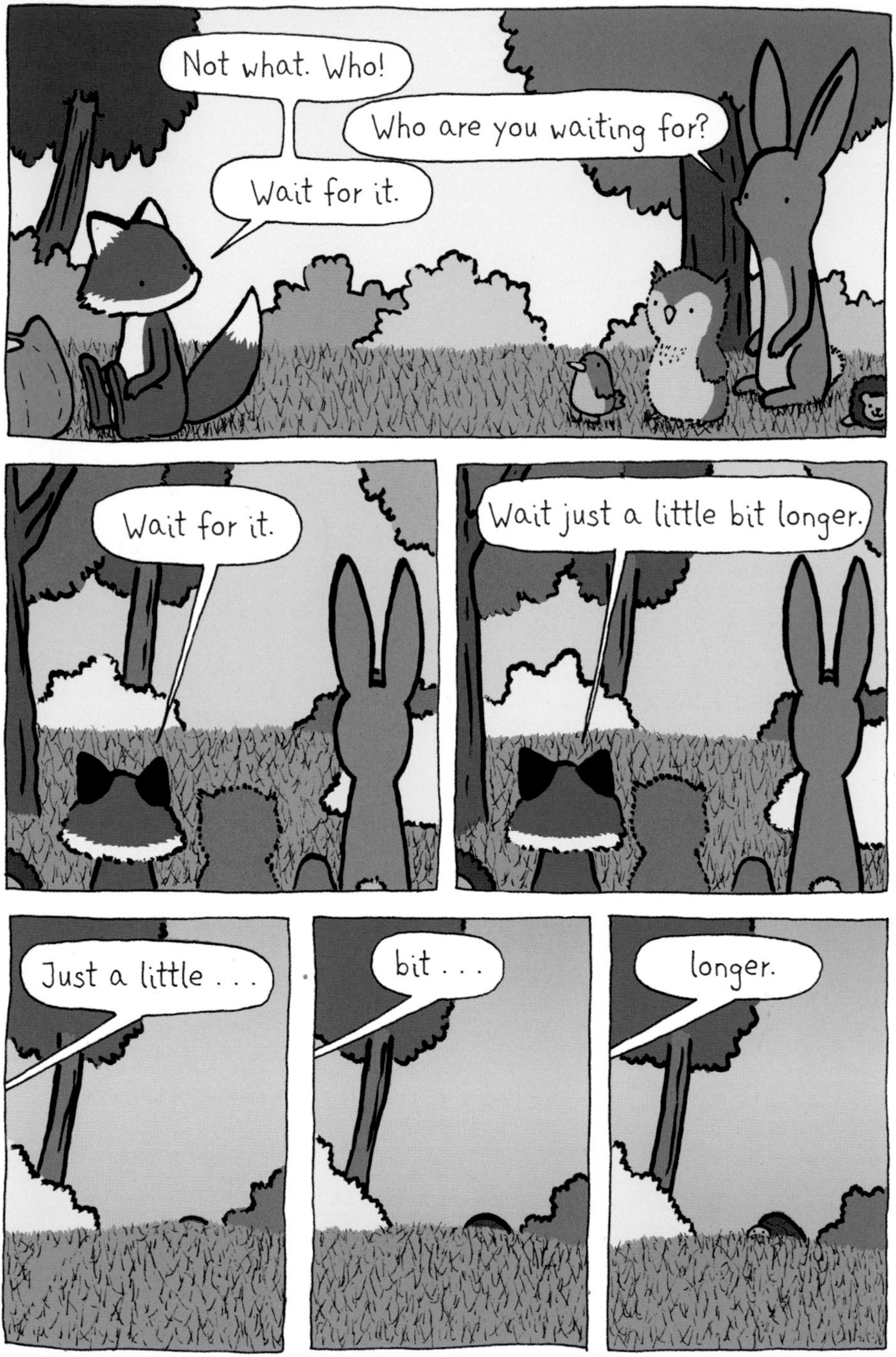
Not what. Who!
Who are you waiting for?
Wait for it.
Wait for it.
Wait just a little bit longer.
Just a little . . .
bit . . .
longer.

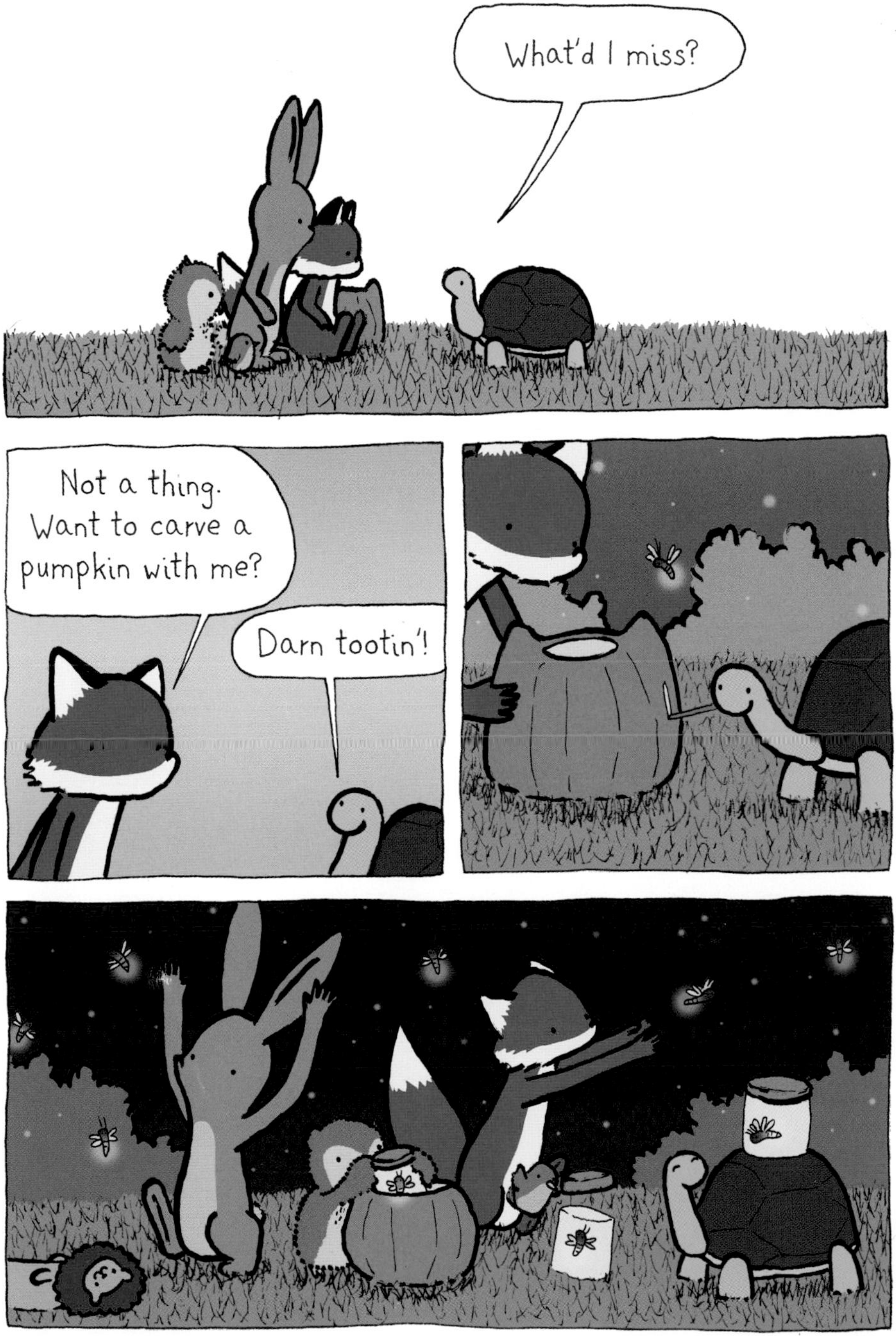
What'd I miss?
Not a thing.
Want to carve a
pumpkin with me?
Darn tootin'!

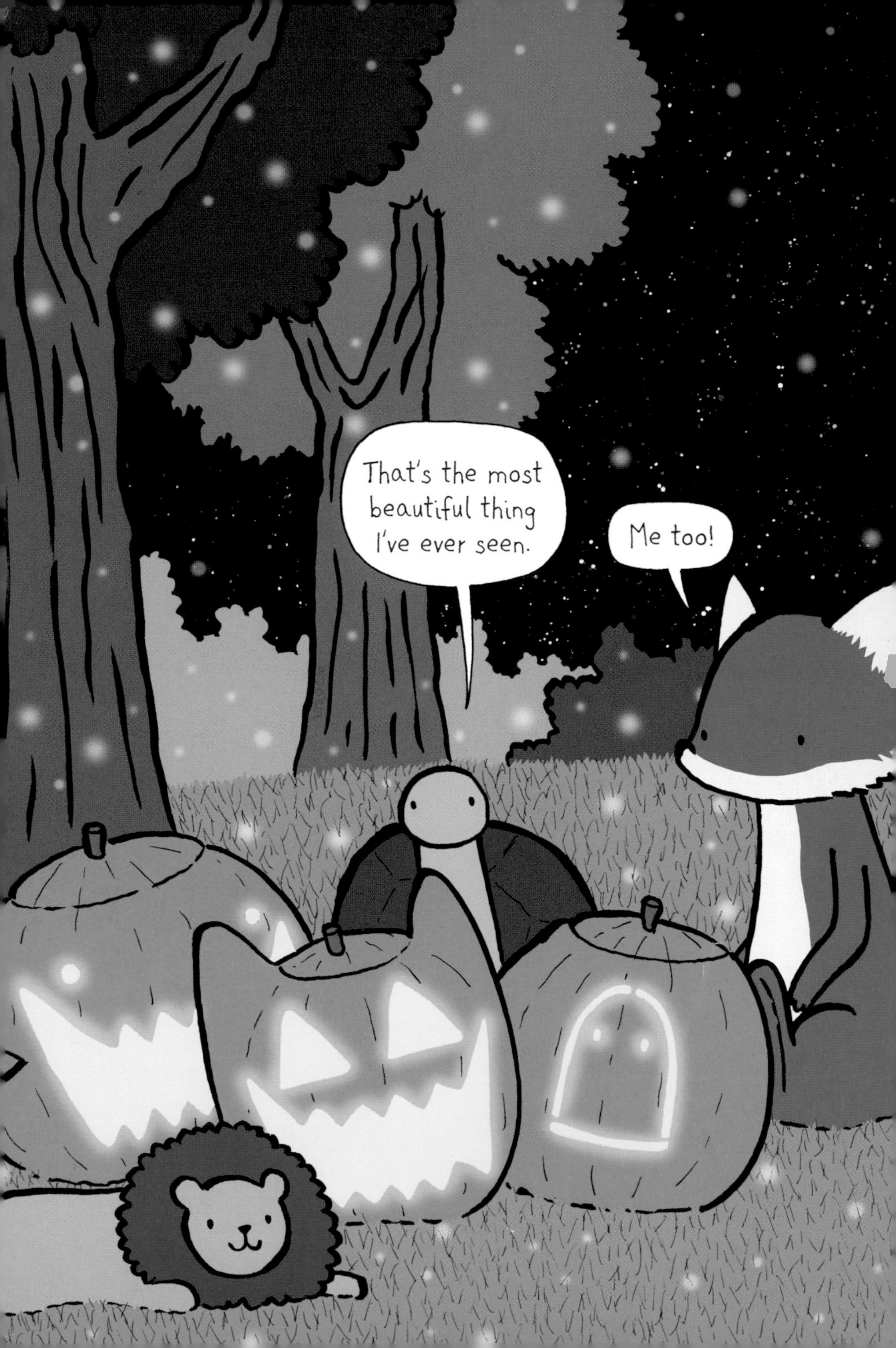
That's the most beautiful thing I've ever seen.
Me too!

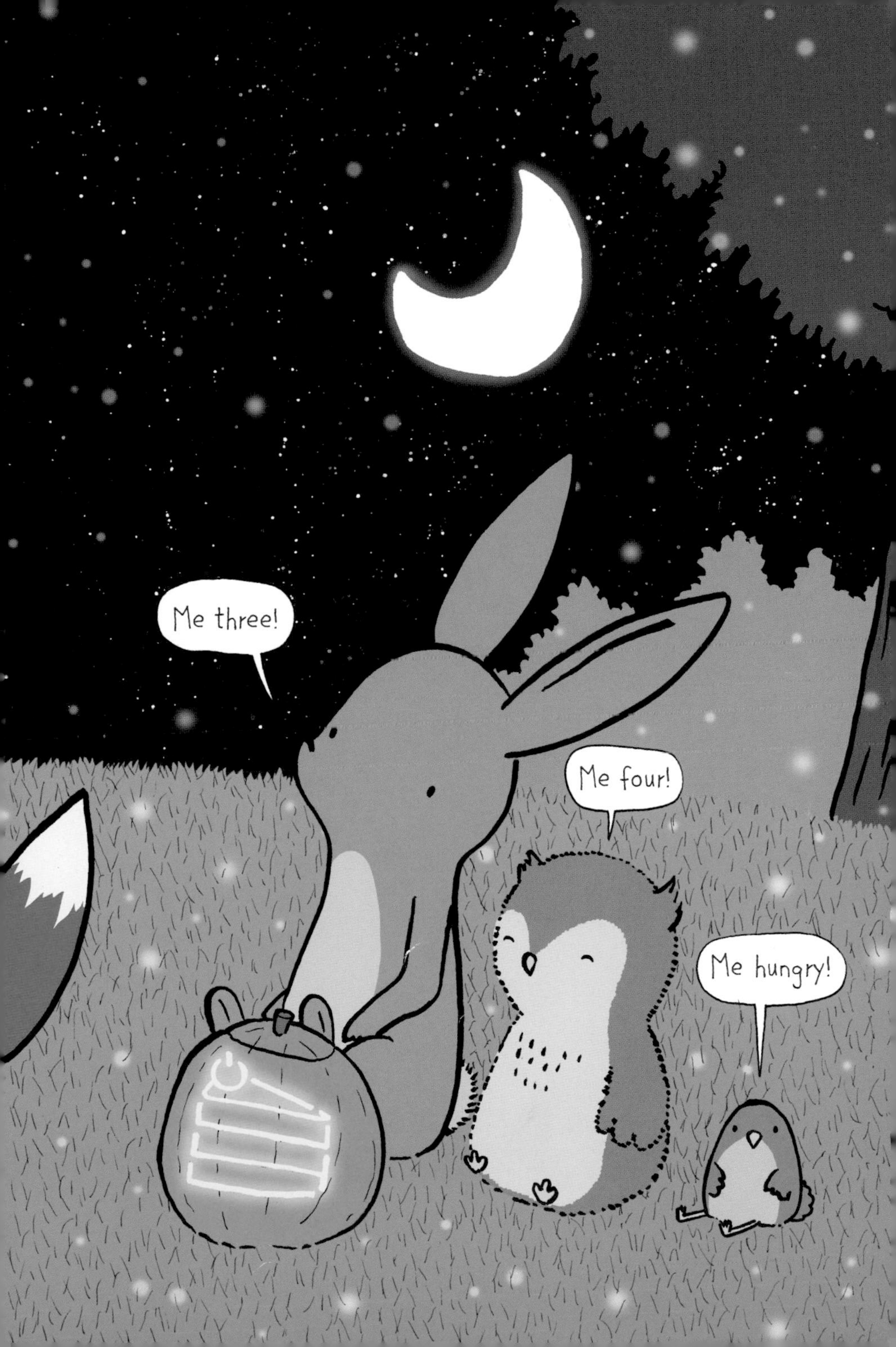
Me three!
Me four!
Me hungry!

ABOUT THE AUTHOR

Beth Ferry only grows pumpkins in her garden, which makes fall her second-favorite season. If she is lucky, her dog will not have eaten all the pumpkins before she's had a chance to carve them—often into characters from her books, which include *The Scarecrow*, *Swashby and the Sea*, and *Stick and Stone*. All these books begin with the letter S, which is Beth's favorite letter because it begins many of her favorite words, including *sunshine*, *sand*, and *sea*. S also begins the words *sweet* and *silly*, which are the main flavors of the world of Fox and Rabbit. Sparrow would argue that sweet and salty are the best flavors, and Beth just might agree. You can learn more at bethferry.com

ABOUT THE ILLUSTRATOR

Gergely Dudás is a self-taught illustrator. He was born in July 1991. His artwork in the early 1990s was a lot more abstract than it is today. He is the creator of the Bear's Book of Hidden Things seek-and-find series.

Like Fox, Rabbit, and Owl, Gergely spent almost every afternoon of his childhood at the playground, playing pretend with his friend Dani. And, like Fox, he loves fall because of the many warm colors that appear on the trees and bushes.

He lives with his girlfriend and a dwarf rabbit called Fahéj.

Gergely's work is inspired by the magic of the natural world. You can see more from him at dudolf.com.

FOR ZACH, WHOSE IMAGINATION IS AN INSPIRATION
—B.F.

FOR MY DEAR FRIEND JANÓ,
WHO LIKES ADVENTURES JUST AS MUCH AS I DO
—G.D.

The art in this book was created with graphite and ink and colored digitally.

PUBLISHER'S NOTE: This is a work of fiction. Names, characters, places, and incidents are either the product of the author's imagination or used fictitiously, and any resemblance to actual persons, living or dead, business establishments, events, or locales is entirely coincidental.

Cataloging-in-Publication Data has been applied for and may be obtained from the Library of Congress.

ISBN 978-1-4197-4687-1

Text copyright © 2020 Beth Ferry
Illustrations copyright © 2020 Gergely Dudás
Book design by Steph Stilwell

Printed and bound in China
10 9 8 7 6 5 4 3 2 1

Amulet Books are available at special discounts when purchased in quantity for premiums and promotions as well as fundraising or educational use. Special editions can also be created to specification. For details, contact specialsales@abramsbooks.com or the address below.

Amulet Books® is a registered trademark of Harry N. Abrams, Inc.

ABRAMS The Art of Books
195 Broadway, New York, NY 10007
abramsbooks.com